MIXED BLESSINGS
AND OTHER LOVE STORIES

MARION LINDSEY-NOBLE

To Pat and Mike
with love.

Marion

22nd June 2013.

Cashmere Publishing

First published in Great Britain in 2013 by
Cashmere Publishing
Brompton Regis
TA22 9NW
Somerset

marion.lindseynoble@btinternet.com

A CIP catalogue record for this book is available
from the British Library

ISBN 978 0 9557932 3 3

Printed and bound in Great Britain by Booksprint

DEDICATION

For my ever patient and generous husband
and best friend with love

CONTENTS

MIXED BLESSINGS

MIXED BLESSINGS

It was a Wednesday and meant to be the happiest day in Patricia's life. To her it felt like the saddest day of them all.

In a few moments she would be getting married. There would not be any shortage of her new husband's family; their numbers could probably fill a small concert hall. They would celebrate and cheer and dance whilst her family would sit at home thinking of her with bitterness, anger and disappointment. This was not how they had imagined their eldest daughter's wedding day. They had saved up for years to give her away in style, to fulfil her dream, the dream of every little girl: a wedding in a country church, wearing a long, elegant white dress, an embroidered lace veil, a little tiara in her blond hair, flower petals thrown over her by excited guests and well-wishers as she came out of church on the arm of the man she loved, a lavish dinner and dance in the grounds of a country mansion to follow...

None of those dreams had come true; not the way they had imagined.

Instead she was alone in the midst of people she barely knew, preparing for a ceremony she hardly understood and surroundings which were alien. The only familiar point of reference would be the man she was about to marry, the charming, handsome and ambitious Amir.

¤ ¤ ¤ ¤ ¤

The reaction of her parents, particularly her father, to her choice of husband had been a complete surprise to her, because he had been a Dad who had doted on his two girls, who had done everything for the first twenty years of their lives to amuse and delight them, to further their interests and to enable both of them to have the best possible education. Patricia's little sister Audrey, only two years younger than her, was studying to be a pharmacist at King's College whilst Patricia had chosen accountancy at St. Mary's, in London. They were both heading to be successful career girls, relegating the thought of marriage and children to the back of their minds in order to make the most of their opportunities.

The end of their time at university was celebrated within their respective circle of friends, and graduation ceremonies were attended by their proud parents. The girls were pleased with themselves that they had managed to spread great happiness in their parent's hearts and vowed to continue to repay their sacrifices.

And then Patricia had met Amir.

◻   ◻   ◻   ◻   ◻

She had only been at Lawson's Accountancy offices for a week when she was introduced to her mentor who would guide her through the workings of the firm and would help her to put the theories of her studies into practice for the good of the company.

Amir was patient, funny – and she had to admit reluctantly – that he was good-looking, too. His thick, black hair was trendily styled and gelled into sticking up on top (a bit like a hedgehog, she thought). He was a natty dresser, insisting on well-tailored suits, designer shirts and shiny hand-made shoes, looking every inch the young star accountant who would go on to great things.

Only later did she find out that the company had been founded by an uncle of his, which explained Amir's self-assurance and fearless approach to decision making. There was some security in nepotism.

12

Apart from his Asian appearance, there was nothing exotic about Amir. He had grown up in London, spoke with a slight Estuary accent and behaved like any young, well brought-up Englishman. He joined everyone on Friday nights for a drink in the pub, met friends for sports or cultural events at the weekends and seemed to eat everything on offer. He would flirt with young ladies, but there were no rumours of a girlfriend.

When asked he would joke that his parents had already chosen a bride when he was three.

Patricia and Amir hit it off straight away. She got used to his dark brown eyes resting rather frequently on her, and was not surprised when he invited her after three months for a lunch time snack; a drink after office hours and finally a dinner on a Friday night. He was even more charming and funny privately as if he had been released from the chains of office etiquette.

They made their dates a regular habit edging slowly towards, what Patricia hoped, would be a more serious relationship.

Office tongues began to wag. When he was called into his uncle's office, Patricia feared that it would be the end of her job or their relationship. Amir never told her what had been said but at the end of their next date he kissed her passionately and they couldn't rush upstairs to her apartment quickly enough to still their physical hunger for each other. It wasn't the thing good girls did, but she hoped that Amir would not hold it against her and consider her reputation sullied. After all, they loved each other, or at least, she loved him.

Needing reassurance, she wheedled out of him that his parents would accept a non-Bengali daughter-in-law; they had tried to match-make several times but he had resisted. Even though they had spent their adult lives in England and, as Amir said, they were 'westernised', he had to concede that most of the time they were clinging on to their own way of life. His mother wore *saris* and was content in her role as a devoted wife without any ambitions for a professional career, while his father had always been the bread-winner leaving the house in the mornings like an English gentleman, but changing into his *lunghi* as soon as he arrived home from work. As far as Amir knew, they had only ever made friends with Bangladeshis, a dignified circle of homesick people who were determined to make their fortune in Britain and to give the next generation a head-start.

It took Amir two months until he plucked up the courage to ask his parents whether he could bring a colleague from work along on one of his Sunday afternoon visits.

Patricia went into a spin, part excited, part anxious. She wanted to get it absolutely right and to make a favourable first impression. She looked in the mirror and saw herself: tall, slim, shoulder-length blond hair, beautifully trimmed by an expensive hairdresser, her big blue eyes framed by stylish glasses. She was used to power-dressing, usually wearing elegant, classy two-piece-suits either with trousers or knee-length skirts, softened by sporty blouses or cashmere sweaters. She would tone down the high heels, though, and wear ballerina pumps instead.

As she had just been promoted to a more senior post, she was confident that she was in every respect an acceptable proposition for any future in-laws.

Amir thought it unnecessary to take presents but Patricia bought a big box of the finest chocolates, just in case.

The young couple had set off to arrive in time for lunch. They drove fast along the M25 in his blue MG. Once they had crossed the Thames, they turned towards the northern outskirts of London. The roads merged into wide and leafy lanes which hinted at countryside close by.

Amir swung the car into a residential side road and stopped outside a large 1930s house. The late summer sun shimmered in the many window panes and kissed the sea of blooms lining the path to the door as if to make up for the damp weeks of late. They parked by the garage door and Amir helped her out of the low seat.

As they approached, the front door opened without a knock. A crowd appeared in the gap, all laughing, his mother, then his father, and when they stepped aside, a young man who could have been Amir's twin. Behind him appeared the happy faces of three pretty young girls in colourful *saris.* Patricia watched the scene with amusement, still standing a few steps behind Amir. When hugs, kisses and cries of delight had abated, they suddenly remembered their guest and turned to Patricia with unconcealed curiosity.

'*Amma,* this is Patricia.'

Patricia smiled and bent down to pay her respects, *salaam,* as Amir had instructed her to do but his mother caught her before she could even fully bend her knees.

'No, no, no, no, no!' she exclaimed shaking her head and making clucking noises, so that the black curls escaped from under her *achol* − the end of her beautifully embroidered sari draped over her head.

'We are in England. No need to do that!'

Patricia sighed inwardly with relief; they really were westernised and broad-minded.

'My father Mohammed, Bulbul, Hemma, Parul and Keema,' Amir introduced his family pointing at each of them standing in a half circle. They shook hands with her and smiled welcomingly. Then the girls took charge of the visitor and gave her a tour of the house. Bulbul monopolised his brother and lead him away from the women.

The welcoming ceremony over, the mother went back into the kitchen from where exotic smells escaped when she opened the door, while the father went into the sitting room back to his Sunday papers.

When Amir's mother called out that lunch was ready, they were ushered into the dining room. The table was set creaking with crockery, glasses and serving dishes, full of beautifully presented Bengali food.

Patricia had by now been to several Indian restaurants with Amir but she had never seen or smelled anything like this. Once she started eating, she was charmed by the balanced seasoning, the combination of spices and herbs; none of the dishes set her tongue on fire as she had feared. It came quite naturally that she ate with her hands, as everyone else around her did, ignoring the cutlery put at her place alone to save her embarrassment. Seeing that gravy was running down her palms and wrists, Mohammed laughed and showed her how it was done properly. Patricia felt the family's appreciative looks; her willingness to adjust broke the ice.

Their stomachs filled, they concentrated on conversation while still nibbling at the sweetmeats rounding off the feast. They were courteous enough to speak in English, only occasionally lapsing into Bengali when the discussion about politics became a little heated.

They asked her a few questions about her family and seemed satisfied with her answers but soon someone butted in and the conversation changed direction.

After lunch Amir professed that he had a lot of work to do to prepare for the coming week. Patrica feared that it might look like an indecently hasty retreat and offered to help clearing the table which looked now like a battle field. However, Amir insisted that they leave and nobody seemed to mind.

'They'll retire to have a nap,' he explained in the car.

Not the women, she thought, unless they have a magic wand to make the mess disappear, stack the dishwasher and soak the stained table cloth which looked now as if it had caught measles.

'It went rather well,' Amir added. 'Well done, you!' He put his hand for a moment on her knee and smiled looking ahead at the motorway, revving the engine for a fast journey home.

¤　　¤　　¤　　¤　　¤

Now it was her turn.

16

Her visits home had become sporadic. To her parents she had excused herself because of a heavy workload and gave the impression that she was entirely focusing on her path up the career ladder. She had mentioned to her sister that there was a man in her life but she knew that until she introduced him to the family they would assume that it wasn't serious.

She knew exactly why she had a lump in her throat when she considered doing so. They would worry. They had heard tales of naive English girls marrying in Turkey or Pakistan who were suddenly expected to become submissive wives and, when they couldn't bear it anymore, had to flee from the husbands leaving their children behind.

But Amir was different; she was convinced of it! It was time to be brave and stand by him!

'Mum,' she rang unexpectedly: 'Can I come at the weekend?'… and before her mother could express her delight, Patricia added: 'and bring someone?'

After a brief hesitation, her mother assured her that of course, she could and that they were looking forward to seeing her and whoever else.

'Who is it?'

'A colleague. His name is Amir.'

'Amir?' her mother repeated as if trying to get this news straight in her mind. Baffled silence followed.

'Yes, he is…'. Before she had finished the sentence, her sister had taken over the telephone and ordered her confused mother to go and make a cup of tea. Patricia heard the kitchen door shut and then the hiss of her sister's whispers:

'Listen, this is not a good time to tell Mum and Dad! We have just come back from a protest march. The council wants to build a mosque between here and Ashford.'

'What has Amir got to do with that?' It was the first time that Patricia had met with less than adoration from her family.

'I would like them to meet my boyfriend, that's all,' she defended herself hotly.

'I see what I can do,' she heard her sister say and a second later the dialling tone screamed into her ear.

'Okay?' Amir asked as she turned round facing him with a fake smile. How could she tell him?

'Yes, fine,' she said brightly, 'it's just that they are in the middle of decorating, so we have to postpone the visit for a bit'.

He seemed relieved that the next weekend would remain their own.

The next weekend, Patricia made up a story that old friends of her parents had sprung a surprise visit on them. After three weeks, her sister still hadn't rung back.

'Dad,' she began with a tremor in her voice having finally managed to pick up enough courage to ring again.

'Hello, poppet,' he sounded his usual self, 'Are you coming to see us soon?'

'Yes Dad, and I would like to bring someone along.'

'Your boyfriend?'

'The thing is, he is English, but his family isn't.'

'What do you mean?' This wasn't going to be easy.

When she had finished explaining, she could hear her father's sharp intake of breath.

'Is he treating you well?'

This was an easy question and she took heart:

'Of course, Daddy. He is very considerate and gentlemanly.'

She had reverted to being his little girl, as if she was asking whether she could go to a party and had to prove that she had made all the necessary arrangements to be safe.

'Well, see you then on Sunday.'

As she put the receiver back in its cradle her heart pounded wildly in her chest.

'We are on,' she announced to Amir more cheerfully than she had been for weeks.

Sunday came and they roared down to Kent in his MG. Patricia had made sure that Amir had the most beautiful big bunch of flowers for her mother and a bottle of her father's favourite Scotch. Her sister would be pleased with a dainty, pink and white silk scarf to wrap elegantly round her neck.

'Let's do battle,' he laughed bravely and rang the doorbell.

Her family must also have stood behind the door awaiting their arrival: It was opened immediately, but instead of hubbub breaking out, they stood rooted to the spot, smiling nervously at each other.

Finally her father took charge and shook Amir vigorously by the hand:

'Welcome, and do come in!'

The distribution of presents helped to thaw the awkwardness, and soon the sisters were chatting animatedly, catching up on news and gossip. The two men, Patricia observed with satisfaction, seemed to have fallen into a deep conversation; she overheard her father enquiring with genuine interest about Amir's family and the country they had come from.

Patricia's mother stood at first loosely around in her sitting room as if lost in her own house, but then she decided to leave them to entertain themselves and disappeared quietly into the kitchen.

'Lunch is ready,' her mother called, emerging and flushed with the effort of cooking. Patricia was touched when she saw the dining table laid out festively in honour of their visit. Usually this only happened at Christmas. Patricia and her mum exchanged glances; they could be confident about the choice of menu as they had put their heads together to work it out, considering the restrictions of a Muslim diet. They had chosen roast leg of lamb, and the rosemary sprigs were now sending heavenly smells ahead of the platter. They knew that Amir loved roast potatoes which were never cooked in his family; the selection of fresh vegetables would round it off nicely. They offered wine to Amir but he refused and preferred orange juice. This had the effect that everyone suddenly professed that they weren't too keen on wine either joining him in having a soft drink. Nothing could go wrong with the desert – a summer pudding; Patricia's favourite.

Patricia noticed with pleasure that Amir polished off every morsel and then leant back in his chair contentedly before complimenting her mother.

So far, so good. The nervous knot in her stomach seemed not quite so tight.

Again, their departure came upon everyone abruptly; Amir declared firmly that he still had some work to do to be ready for the new week. Patricia felt sorry for her parents but assured them that the visit had been immensely successful and thanked them for their tremendous effort with warm hugs.

¤   ¤   ¤   ¤   ¤

Time moved on. Amir was further promoted to chief accountant of the company with a pleasing rise in salary.

They were still not living together, but she was convinced that it was only a matter of time that he would propose. She began to joke that she could see herself quite happily as a spinster, but Amir didn't find it funny, and so she stopped.

And then, one Sunday, he insisted that she should go shopping with a friend as he wished to meet with his parents alone.

'Do you mind us meeting in your flat?' Amir asked. 'It's closer for them.'

'No, of course not! You have got a key.'

Luckily, she had spent the previous weekend giving the rooms a spring clean. She felt confident there was nothing to embarrass her or them.

When she returned, they were sitting on her settee, fidgeting and their faces mirroring doubt as if they couldn't make up their minds what position they should be in. The atmosphere was strangely leaden until Amir's mother heaved herself out of the deep sofa and walked across the room to embrace her.

'Welcome into our family!'

Patricia was speechless for a moment but then joined in with the general hugging and kissing.

'It will be a traditional wedding.' Three pairs of eyes rested upon her.

'Yes, of course.' Patricia was a little confused about the signals Amir's gaze and tone of voice sent out; something of a warning.

'A traditional Bengali wedding; a Muslim wedding,' he explained, watching her reaction. He had emphasized every word to underline its importance as if she was a slow learner.

Patricia wasn't sure what a traditional Muslim wedding entailed but she imagined it was similar to a Christian one, maybe in a mosque instead of a church, and most probably the guests would be dressed in a more exotic fashion.

'That's fine! It will be lovely,' she said and was relieved to see their faces relax. Amir's mother hugged her again before announcing that they would leave, now that things were settled to everyone's satisfaction.

'I shall begin with the preparations immediately, invitations, venue, catering. I'll speak to the Imam tomorrow.' She really was in full flow and would have continued to elaborate had not her husband dragged her away.

'That's Mum. You made her really happy. She will be unstoppable from now on. Brace yourself!' Amir laughed.

Later it occurred to Patricia that Amir had neither asked her or her parents for her hand in marriage but had secured the all-important permission from his parents first.

Still, Patricia was blissfully happy that at last she would be Amir's wife.

Her childhood dream of being a bride in white had vanished but did it matter?

¤   ¤   ¤   ¤   ¤

Her parents had half expected an announcement but they were horrified at the prospect of an Islamic wedding.

'I don't know much about Islam but aren't they allowed to have four wives?' her mother wailed. 'And when he had enough of you he can simply divorce you by saying so three times, and the children will stay with the father.'

'Amir is not like that,' Patricia broke an awkward minute of silence, 'and the wedding is just for show, to make his parents happy.'

'What about making us happy?' Her mother nearly screamed the word 'us' and began to sob uncontrollably.

'Couldn't you find a nice English boy among the millions?'

Her father took Patricia by her shoulders and said sadly:

'I think you better go now. We'll think things over.'

With that he led her to the door.

A week later it was suggested via the telephone that they could have both: They would all turn up for the Islamic wedding, and shortly before or after, Patricia's parents would organise the Christian wedding – the best of both worlds.

Patricia thought it a brilliant idea and was proud of her parents' generosity although she feared that the number of her Bengali in-laws might stretch their budget to its limits.

However, Amir wouldn't hear of it. He didn't even submit the idea to his parents.

She rang home again, politely relating Amir's objections, trying to sound as if it really didn't matter to her, and neither should it matter to them. All she asked them was to be happy for her and to be her moral support on the day.

She was met with stony silence and a clipped: 'No. Do stand up for us, Patricia!'

¤   ¤   ¤   ¤   ¤

She only related the bare bones to Amir, not wanting to paint her parents in a bad light. Nevertheless, he was incensed at how much they had managed to upset her. When he hugged her, her sorrow dissolved into tears and she sobbed into his broad shoulder.

'They'll come round,' he consoled her, not entirely convinced himself and secretly hoping that they wouldn't, the way they felt about him.

Elaborate wedding invitations had gone out, but two weeks later, she still didn't have a reply from her parents.

The suspense weaved itself through the wedding preparations like a venomous snake. Patricia couldn't get rid of the heavy heart and bitter taste in her mouth. She reached a point where she felt anger; anger at her parents' blinkered stubbornness; anger at throwing a large spanner onto her path to happiness, anger that they spoiled this most wonderful time in her life; and embarrassment at having to admit to Amir that her family did not approve of mixed marriages. It looked so bad!

The result was that Patricia felt herself move away from her English background and eagerly integrated in the way of life Amir's family represented. Eventually, the gulf became so wide that she lost the courage to ring home, and even the occasional calls from her sister trying to mediate stopped altogether.

¤   ¤   ¤   ¤   ¤

As she looked at herself now in the mirror, dressed in her blood red sari with lavish gold threads woven into it, her face made up in the style of a Bollywood film star to the point where she hardly recognised herself, and her ears and neck laden with gold and precious stones, she felt that her family had let her down.

She decided there and then that she was going to cut them out of her life and to begin a new one with her husband.

She tore up the congratulatory card, which had arrived this morning and threw it into the waste paper basket. Soon her sisters-in-law would storm into her room to usher her to the festivities.

For the rest of the day, she was immersed in the activities of getting married, at first in a separate room from Amir until they were joined together to thunderous applause.

They were absolutely exhausted but brimming with happiness when they retired. They had planned a short lull between the hectic celebrations and the departure for their honeymoon destination, Bangladesh. It was Amir's duty to introduce his new wife to the family back home.

The honeymoon turned into a strangely exotic time. She had never been to Asia and found it somehow difficult to find her bearings. She regretted that she didn't speak Bengali and had to sit often in on animated conversations without being able to understand or participate. By the time, people talked in English all the arguments of the discussion had been raked over and she was left with small talk. In truth, she felt alien and lonely and breathed a sigh of relief when the aeroplane took off from the bumpy runway of Dhaka airport.

The young couple tried to hold on to the glow of the recent joyful events, but were quickly sucked back into London's world of accountancy. Patricia was left behind by Amir's rise to directorship and concentrated more on making their new house – a wedding present from his family, only five minutes from theirs – homely and comfortable. She loved her new role and when she found out that she was pregnant, she gave gladly into her mother-in-law's suggestion that she should sacrifice her career.

Patricia hadn't heard from her parents and sister since her wedding day, but she couldn't help herself sending them secretly one of the many ornate announcements when her daughter Reeta was born.

Maybe a grandchild could mend bridges?

'I won't hold my breath,' Patricia thought, and indeed she heard nothing.

¤   ¤   ¤   ¤   ¤

The shrill sound of the telephone cut through a leisurely Sunday afternoon while Patricia was playing on the carpet with little Reeta, now almost three years old. Amir sat on the sofa close to them reading the Sunday papers. Patricia threw a glance at her husband and realised that he didn't want to be disturbed. She got up to take the call.

'Hello?' she said, still drowsy with concentration on her daughter's wooden puzzle.

There was a pause before a timid and gruff voice appeared at the other end: 'It's me, Audrey.'

'Oh Sis!' exclaimed Patricia. To her surprise it was pure joy to hear the familiar voice.

'It's Mum...'

'What's wrong, Audrey? Tell me...'

'She has cancer. She is in hospital. She wants to see you.'

Audrey's words came out like bullets from a machine gun, each hurting more than the other.

'Hold on. What sort of cancer? Since when? What's the prognosis?' Patricia had so many questions.

'She was fighting it for a few months last year, but it returned and now it's too advanced...'

'You mean it's terminal?'

'Yes.' The short answer fell into the silence like a heavy rock.

'Are you sure she wants to see me? I don't want to make things worse...'

'So you don't want to see her then?'

'Of course, I want to see her. I have never ever wanted this to happen. I missed you all dreadfully!'

'You better come soon!'

Amir drove her to the hospital the following day with Reeta firmly belted into her child seat. Patricia had come to bring hope and peace, and she had no idea that it would be the last day of her mother's life.

When she entered the hospital room, she found her father

standing in the corner by the window, shrunken and miserable, staring out with unseeing eyes, ignoring the visitors. There was only one bed in the room and her mother's pale face had melted into the pristine white pillows. When Patricia entered, her mother's arms, lying limply on top of the duvet by her sides, indicated a welcome, patting a spot where her eldest should sit.

'Hi Dad.' He only nodded.

'Where is Audrey?'

'Downstairs, having a coffee.'

Patricia sat down as close to her mum as she dared and gave her a gentle hug.

'Lovely to see you, Poppet!' Patricia lip-read.

She cupped the limp hand with both of hers. It was cold and fragile. She brought it to her lips and planted a kiss.

'I am so sorry, Mum!...' All the pent up tears burst the dam of her composure.

'So am I.' Her mother had to push the words out in staccato as if she was choking on them.

'Did you bring Reeta?' She had to breathe heavily between syllables but her eyes revealed the urgency her voice couldn't express.

'Yes, she is downstairs with Amir.'

'Call them.'

Patricia thought she had misheard. 'Them? You mean Reeta?' She needed to be sure to get it right.

'...and her dad,' her mother said with as much determination as she could muster. It exhausted her, and she closed her eyes.

27

Patricia turned in great haste, mumbling: 'I'll be back in a minute,' She didn't wait for the lift but flew down the stairs, not wanting to lose one precious second.

Amir was reluctant to face his mother-in-law. But how could he refuse the wish of a dying woman?

Patricia shepherded her little family to her mother's bedside when, to her surprise, she and her father were ordered out by the rallying patient.

Patricia never knew what had gone on in the sick room after she had shut the door. Her husband remained quiet and subdued afterwards, and when they had returned to their home, Reeta showed off a beautiful medallion on a chain round her neck.

'Grandma in there,' the little girl declared putting her hand over it as if in charge of protecting a great treasure.

'Will you show me?'

Reeta nodded gravely as if to indicate that Mummy was one of the few privileged exceptions.

Patricia unhooked the tiny lock and put the necklace onto the dining table's cloth. The locket sprung open and a miniature version of her mother in happy times smiled out. For balance, there was also a picture of her father happily grinning into the camera standing in his vegetable plot.

¤　¤　¤　¤　¤

Patricia helped her father arrange the funeral and, when she asked Amir timidly − he had every right to object − whether she could reinstate regular visits to keep an eye on him, he had a surprise in store.

'Of course, you can visit him as often as you like, but it would make more sense if he came to stay with us. Tell him to come for the weekend and we shall see where we go from there.'

She hadn't hugged her husband with as much passion for a while. The sadness about the estrangement and her mother's untimely death gently evaporated and was replaced by gratitude and the firm conviction that she had been right after all to marry this man.

It took some convincing the old chap, but her sister Audrey, who now lived with her boyfriend, helped to change his mind.

'I'll miss my garden...' her father grumbled as his daughter and grand-daughter picked him up with his few belongings.

'Would you like to plant a kitchen garden for us?'

'Could do... But I won't eat hot and spicy!'

Patricia laughed: 'You won't have to. I use an awful lot of Mum's recipes.'

'And I won't wear funny clothes!'

'Neither do we.'

Patricia understood: He just wanted to make his position clear, before – to his astonishment – he gave into a feeling of great satisfaction and relief.

NOOR

NOOR

'So, what happened?' I ask my old friend Noor.

We are sitting at a round table of the pavement café in a leafy suburb of London. The sun is shining, the blue and white chequered table cloths spread a holiday atmosphere, we are sipping on iced tea and I am so happy − I haven't seen Noor for thirty years.

I dropped everything when she rang this morning and asked whether I wanted to meet up with her. What a question!

She still wears her hair in a black bob which is now streaked with silver. Her clothes, however, are less expensively flamboyant than they used to be; more of the understated, elegant variety from the High Street; the rings on her hands are still the same without any additions.

She laughs her raucous laugh which has acquired an even more honey-on-gravel rasp over the years. Her laughter has always been her most attractive feature.

With her hooked nose, thin lips and small eyes she was never conventionally pretty in spite of the expensive beauty products she could afford as the daughter of wealthy Ismaili parents. Their riches alone would have made it easy to marry Noor off but their first born had other ideas: She was wilful, self-confident and took full advantage of her family's liberal attitudes.

The last time I had seen Noor, 30 years ago, she had wailed almost hysterically, overcome by sorrow. I can still picture the scene: mascara forming dark rivulets down her cheeks; her usually stylishly coiffed hair hanging in strands around her blotched face; even the Armani suit had lost its beauty and had hung around her bony figure like a protective skin.

'He will never marry me now?' she had sobbed and I hadn't known how to console her except with platitudes. She had been my friend and I had let her down.

Noor's home had been in a part of London only inhabited by the wealthy. Her family had revamped the Victorian mansion according to their refined tastes and needs. The ample garden with manicured lawns, framed by mature trees and English flower borders, were maintained by two full-time gardeners. Apart from occasionally cutting roses for a vase, the family were not really involved in its upkeep.

The inside of the house boasted thick Persian carpets on highly polished oak floors. The almost white settees were livened up by colourful Indian cushions which were sprinkled with tiny glittering silver disks, or had little mirrors delicately sown into stencilled holes. There were elaborate chandeliers in each room dripping from the ceilings. Glass cabinets of polished mahogany displayed precious crystal glasses and pricey porcelain figurines by famous potteries, obviously a much loved collection of somebody in the family. Some holiday souvenirs from various parts of the world and from pilgrimages to holy Muslim places jostled incongruously with the more expensive pieces.

There was also a strangely eclectic collection of African artefacts strewn throughout the house. According to Noor, they evoked painful but sweet memories of the family's privileged past in Uganda from where they had been expelled by the vindictive and cruel Idi Amin in 1972. Only after pestering her for more information did Noor confirm that they had owned a chain of hotels and many of the coffee plantations which they had to leave behind to start a new life as refugees in England.

Being Ismailis, they were not suppressed for long. Instead, they channelled their energies and some funds, they had managed to rescue ahead of their departure, into building up new, successful businesses. They could rely on the network, assistance and spirit of the Ismaili community. By the time I met Noor, her family lived a lavish life style again, and the women were happy with their westernised identities, occupying themselves mainly with charity lunches, beauty treatments and shopping trips.

Noor loved her family and the carefree life they provided. She dabbled in various privately paid study courses but nothing so serious that it would disrupt her social calendar. On the odd occasion when she was asked to sit an examination, she went to pieces with nerves and finally opted out altogether claiming illness and collecting sympathetic embraces from her mother and siblings. Her father, used to his gaggle of emotional females, simply laughed, reminding his eldest daughter that there really was no need to sit exams; she would marry a wealthy boy who would take care of her as he had taken care of her mother and his five daughters.

I had met Noor for the first time when she was with Vikram, a university friend of my boyfriend from whom I separated soon afterwards. Vikram seemed nice enough, and they looked happy together, if a little ill-matched: She with her attire from designer shops in Bond Street and he in down-market jeans and a cheap nylon shirt in a sickly shade of yellow.

A few weeks later, I invited them to my council house for dinner. It was a complicated affair as Noor's diet was not only restricted by religious considerations but by the fact that she was a fussy eater. Her boyfriend turned out to be a Hindu from Mauritius, who preferred vegetarian meals. The only safe and acceptable menu, I worked out, was cauliflower cheese and roast potatoes. Desert was easier: I opted for a Turkish Delight syllabub with rose and orange flower waters which turned out to be a great success.

I didn't see Noor for several weeks until she suddenly turned up at my doorstep in floods of tears, the glamorous red lipstick smeared over the corners of her mouth.

'Come on in,' wasn't even necessary as she barged past me into the corridor.

'I don't know what to think,' she cried throwing herself into my lumpy, worn sofa, dislodging the dark-blue Indian throw which I had carefully draped across its shiny and bald patches.

'Have a cup of tea,' I pushed the one I had just made for myself into her hand and she began to sip greedily.

'Now start at the beginning and tell me all about him,' I encouraged her.

She recapped how she had met Vikram at a family do. It had been arranged by her cousin who had studied law and politics in London in the same year. Soon afterwards her family had an inkling that she was dating someone but she had only vaguely pointed him out on one of the blurred photographs from the party. She certainly hadn't told them that he was a Hindu and – on a grant. Looking tall and distinguished with an unsmiling, grave face, Vikram had done or said nothing to mislead them when introduced; however, no one had – and he was fully unaware of this – doubted his suspected favourable credentials and well-to-do background. Why else would Noor have invited him? And she was not the one to disillusion them!

So there she had sat on my old settee, the throw bunched up around her, gasping in exasperation and sorrow:

'We have been going out now for over a year and he still hasn't said anything!'

I must have looked baffled because she added... 'anything about our future together...about getting married, I mean!'

'Give it time.'

'After more than a year?' she was tearfully outraged. 'I keep refusing perfectly good marriage proposals and I can't keep my family at bay forever.'

It was an alien world to me. I had always chosen my lovers myself and it would never have occurred to me to put any of them under pressure, however much I had longed for a commitment.

If love wasn't declared naturally it wasn't worth having.

'He knows I love him and I want him but he keeps retreating whenever I mention it.' It was new to her that there were things – like love – which couldn't be bought or forced.

I supressed a smile. To my mind she was going about it in exactly the wrong way. Poor, persecuted Vikram! He must have felt something for her otherwise he would have fled long ago.

'Just give it a little more time,' I repeated feebly, not hopeful that she would take my advice. She was obviously used to getting what she wanted.

'Can you speak to him?' I thought I hadn't heard properly

'But I hardly know him!' I protested. Now that she had stated her plan, she was determined that at least she would win that particular battle.

'I'll try,' I sighed and capitulated almost immediately.

¤   ¤   ¤   ¤   ¤

'Vikram, it's Rosemary, Nick's ex-girlfriend.'

'Oh hi there!' he said through the telephone in impeccable, almost accent-free English.

'How are you?' he enquired politely.

'I'm fine,' I said, wishing fervently to come to the point of my call: 'Vikram, can we meet up and have a chat?'

'Certainly. It will be nice to see you again. What is it about?' He sounded intrigued.

'It's difficult on the phone...' I stuttered.

'Okay, shall we say tomorrow lunchtime in the student bar?'

'Great,' I feigned enthusiasm. I knew exactly where the student bar was; Nick and I had been there many times.

'Tomorrow, one o'clock at the student bar,' I confirmed; 'I'll be there!'

As it happened, we only met for half an hour. I was unusually tongue-tied and felt that it wasn't really my place to talk to Vikram about his relationship with Noor. He was kind, realising my predicament from my stumbling words. At least I got a promise out of him that he would talk to Noor directly.

'You are a good friend to Noor and I appreciate that,' he said while warmly shaking my hand.

¤   ¤   ¤   ¤   ¤

The next time I saw them they were together, inseparable, happily smiling, Noor almost ecstatically joyful.

During the following few months, I was invited several times to family gatherings or parties in Noor's house – elaborate affairs attended by beautifully dressed people, mainly members of the Ismaili community of London. Lavish buffets offered wonderful square meals in addition to my meagre dole money fare.

Vikram was never there, claiming to prepare for examinations. I suspected, Noor still hadn't told her family the truth about him, and he hadn't proposed. What sort of truce they had arranged, I knew not.

'How are things going between you and Vikram?' I asked when we were both standing at the buffet nibbling on plump vegetable *samosas*.

'Fine,' she said with forced jollity and a hint of resignation.

'What will you do once he has finished his degree course?' It was a question which made her visibly uncomfortable.

Her 'Don't know,' sounded more like: 'Don't want to know.' She shrugged her shoulders and returned to the party.

Soon afterwards, I finally found a job in another town. I never met Noor and Vikram again in spite of sending them my new contact details.

That is, until about a year later, when she stood outside my new address in hysterics.

Not again!

'He will never marry me now!'

After a cup of calming camomile tea, several more outbursts of sobbing, brought under control by warm hugs, I needed to get to the bottom of her initial statement:

'What has happened now?'

'Nothing happened – that's the whole point!' she was about to burst into tears again.

'Just tell me the latest. Have you finally introduced him properly to your family?'

She shook her head sadly. 'I can't if he doesn't propose.'

'That's pathetic, Noor! He is a nice man, intelligent, with good prospects and most of all, he loves you.'

'I am not so sure.'

'After all this time? Why not?' I was getting irritated..

'He doesn't want to be introduced to my family. He hasn't ever mentioned me to his mother in Mauritius and his student visa is running out in two month.'

'So what are you waiting for?' I must have sounded impatient.

'I proposed to him yesterday,' she dropped the bombshell in a sheepish whisper, stunned at her own audacity..

'And?' I was holding my breath.

'He refused.' She burst into tears again.

I nearly exploded: It was like mediating between two stubborn teenagers!

'He said that if he had any intention of marrying me, he would have proposed long ago. Then he went on about that he was never going to earn enough money to give me the lifestyle I was used to.'

'That's probably true. What did you say?'

'That I had plenty of money for both of us.' She had felt very proud of her solution but he hadn't taken kindly to it:

'Do you seriously think that I will be kept by my wife and her family? If you think that you don't know me at all!'

Poor Noor had been completely baffled by this outburst and had waited for him to suggest something more acceptable, when he said to her horror: 'I shall go back home next month, work my way up and look after my widowed mother. I have neglected her for far too long. It's the only life I can offer and I know it won't be enough for you; so we better call it a day.'

◻ ◻ ◻ ◻ ◻

Thirty years later, I am about to hear whether their story had ended there. We both lean in towards the middle of the table as if plotting a conspiracy:

'Vikram did return home,' Noor sighs theatrically. 'Of course, I was distraught and frantic and behaving like a lunatic. My parents worried themselves sick when they noticed that I had lost a lot of weight; I was depressed most of the time and avoided company. They had no idea why. Finally, I owned up and told them about my love affair with Vikram. I also told them about his limited professional prospects, where he lived, and that he was a Hindu.'

'At last!' I clap my hands.

Noor looks at me disapprovingly:

'It was the hardest thing I ever had to do!' I believe her.

After the first shock had worn off, the parents conceded that it must be true love. How could they deny their beloved daughter lifelong happiness? They even openly acknowledged a begrudging respect to the man who had behaved in such an unusually principled and honourable fashion.

Even amongst their broadminded Ismaili friends there were not many who agreed with them.

'I wrote to him,' Noor now smiles all over her face as if it had happened only yesterday, 'and he replied immediately though cautiously, warning me that life would be a lot harder than it was in my sheltered haven in London; but he admitted that he had missed me more than he had expected. That was it! I didn't mind where I would live with him, even if it was in a dog kennel.' I had my doubts but her eyes glinted in triumph.

'I bought my flight,' she continued, 'and went with the blessings of my parents, promising to return, should things not work out. At the airport, they gave me an open return flight ticket which I hoped I would never have to use.'

This was the new, courageous Noor I had never known.

'My whole family came out for the wedding; that was a wonderful surprise! They actually bought us a house as a wedding gift,' she laughs. 'Vikram was furious but he loves the house as much as I do.'

'So, how is life?' I enquire.

41

'Great! Well, I couldn't have children, but we adopted two local ones, a boy and a girl, Jay and Nasma; they are now at London University and are staying with one of my sisters. That's why I am here, to visit them. Vikram carved out a good career in the Mauritian Civil Service, and I do some charity work – environment and children are my specialities.'

I know it's none of my business but I am curious:

'Does your family still support you?'

She laughs: 'I do exploit their generosity occasionally but any contributions go straight into the charity coffers!'

Noor a doting wife, mother and self-less charity worker? I am amazed.

'Were you accepted easily in Mauritius?'

'Nothing mattered except being with Vikram. Of course, he was sceptical whether I would adjust once the novelty had worn off. I had to work hard to be accepted and of course, I made the occasional social gaffe, but I wanted my husband to be proud of me and the more I succeeded the more I enjoyed myself.'

She sits back in her chair smiling smugly. Her bangles tinkle while she tucks her hair behind each ear. Even her features have softened.

And then she adds with triumph: 'After a few years, the tables turned and we were hailed as a good example of tolerance and respect.'

How wonderful! She not only has won the battle for her man, she has single-handedly proven to all the doubters that true love does conquer all.

'Come on, let's go. I'll introduce you to my children...'she laughs that throaty, cheeky laugh.

'And next year you must come out to Mauritius and stay with us.'

I might just do that.

KIP

KIP

I don't recognise the woman sitting opposite me, wringing her hands, tears streaming down her pale, careworn face from eyes underlined by genuine black rings like smudged kohl.

She is young if one can judge from her translucent skin but she sits on my sofa like an old woman, bent and morose. It's not a visit to lighten up my day.

I am going to miss my Bingo session now; I am really annoyed having to let my friend Philomena down. I call her 'Phil'; it's shorter and friendlier. Whatever was her mother thinking of giving her that name!

Phil will probably pop in after the Bingo session to check that I'm alright. I hope that young woman will be gone by then.

I should take some interest in this pathetic figure shrouded in a black, flowing cloth covering up her entire shape including the top of her head. I don't mind long skirts, over the knees, or flowery ones down to the ankles like the Hippies used to wear. I really think the young generation has gone too far the other way showing off parts of their bodies that should better stay hidden; shameless, some of them!

But this young lady is overdoing 'modesty'. The only thing visible is this pale face, like a sad full moon, and the tips of her dirty toes in worn-out, clumpy sandals peeping out from underneath the hem like barbecued chipolatas which have fallen into the ashes.

I have no way of knowing what she is wearing underneath; I hope some thermals because this cloak would not have protected her on the way to my house through the icy wind and rain on this winter afternoon.

Her name is Keeley. I remember that much, but the rest of her I don't know; last I had heard of her she had shortened her name to KIP, just her initials Keeley Isla Peters. It was meant to be cool.

How her mother had agonised over the choice of names for the baby, and how proud she had been to come up with this!

I knew Keeley Isla, but I never got to know KIP – I didn't really want to.

I only heard occasionally through the grape vine that KIP was in trouble one way or another. I rarely think about that time now. It is too painful. I prefer to remember Keeley, the cute little girl with her big, blue, questioning eyes and blond, curly hair standing away from her head like the rays running off the sun in one of her nursery paintings.

'Shall I make you a cup of tea?' My question interrupts whatever she is thinking.

The young woman shakes her head slowly as if it was fastened to her neck by tight elastics allowing only restricted movement.

'A glass of water?' I persist.

'Yes, please,' she whispers as if someone has disconnected her breath from her voice box.

I go to the kitchen, let the tab run until the water feels fresh and cool. I fill a tumbler and carry it back to my sitting room. Before I can place it on the coaster on the little table next to the sofa she stretches out her hand from underneath the bat-like wing of her robe. I shudder. I don't want to be horrible, but it's eerie, like the arm of a corpse emerging from the grave in a horror film.

'Thank you,' she says gratefully.

I am a little taken aback because Keeley had never been a child who took easily to saying her 'pleases' and 'thank-yous'. In fact, if I remember rightly, the last time I had anything to do with her, she told me to … well, you get the drift.

'You want to take that cloak off? It must be uncomfortable.'

Again, she shakes her head without looking at me pulling it tighter around her as if for protection. For the first time, I notice that she has put on weight.

I don't understand how she can wear this stuff. It makes her look like a crow.

There was a time when I bought sweet paisley patterned dresses for her. Her mother made her wear them whenever they came to visit me, but Keeley was always more of a tomboy and looked in them as if she was wearing them under duress. So I stopped.

Keeley hadn't been a menacing child but there was something wild about her. It was a simple case of 'nature loading the gun and nurture pulling the trigger': Keeley's mother, my daughter Claire, had no husband and a baby by another useless boyfriend who left after the first sleepless night. I must give her credit though, she did pull herself together after a few chaotic months on benefits and worked her way up from Girl Friday to manageress of a travel agency.

Claire was very proud of herself, but of course, she had not much time for her children. As soon as anybody would have them, they were dumped with child minders or kind neighbours; and later on, after-school clubs and classes. To my mind, Keeley learnt quickly to play up one adult against another, everyone thinking she was safely ensconced elsewhere but not being in any of the places as planned.

Her mother used to complain that when she herself really made an effort at the weekends to do something with the kids,

Keeley never willingly participated, not even in activities like hikes, games, parties or whatever. That child was detached like a house in the middle of nowhere doing her own thing, either in her room, which she was known to barricade or, God-knows-where, away from home. Before you could say: 'but don't go far and be back in an hour,' she was gone, wordlessly gone; most of the time not just for an hour. I would have understood if there had been Gypsy blood in her family but her mother was always as settled as a deep-rooted tree, which was the trouble because her toy boys didn't want to live like that.

'So what's the matter, Keeley?' I ask now.

She is as surprised to hear her real name as I am saying it out loud. I half expect her to correct me and to insist on KIP but she doesn't. Things must be bad!

'Can I stay ... for a few days?' she whispers to her shrouded knees.

I nearly fall off my chair.

'Why?' I reply defensively.

'I need to disappear for a bit.'

'Are you in trouble with the police again? Because if you are, I shall go straight away....'

Her head seems to have loosened from the entangled elastic and is now violently swinging from left to right in denial.

'No, no, nothing like that.'

It is not reassuring.

'Keeley, I haven't seen hide nor hair of you for years. In fact, the last time I saw you I remember you being very rude to me, and I had sworn to myself that I would wash my hands off you.' My stare is a warning that I will not be giving in this time.

'I know… and I am sorry.' It doesn't sound contrite, more resigned and exasperated with her own stupidity. She sighs deeply.

'So who is after you?'

'My husband.'

'What?… How old are you now?'

'I know… I am eighteen… and I am pregnant.'

'Holy Mary, are you mad?'

There is no answer to that and we both sit avoiding each other's eyes, our brains working overtime to adjust to the news.

'So why is he after you?'

'He thinks I want to leave him.'

'And do you?'

'I am not sure. I just want a little bit more freedom.'

Yes, freedom was the anthem of Keeley's teenage years. Everything and everybody was in her way, restricting her until she restricted herself – involuntarily, of course.

At first it was school, those stupid teachers who couldn't teach her anything. Then she got into a gang of horrible girls who taught her how to truant; Keeley didn't mind learning that sort of thing, in fact she did quite well at it. She drove her mother mad because she was constantly called to school, reprimanded that she couldn't keep control of her daughter, and finally being threatened with legal action.

But to be fair, her mother tried everything: talking to Keeley, appealing to her sense of fairness, pleading for understanding and requesting not to make things worse for her mother and herself. What else was she supposed to do? After all, she had to go to work, plus she had another child to look after.

Keeley couldn't see the wave of helplessness engulfing her mother. They had never been close and it came back to haunt them.

Finally, a last shred of decency – buried somewhere deeply in her soul – told Keeley that everybody would be better off if she disappeared.

There were rumours that she lived on the streets of a nearby town; then she supposedly joined an all-girls gang and took shelter with one of its members who seemed to have free run of her home.

To everybody's surprise, she suddenly turned up on my doorstep after several weeks, professing that she had changed her mind and did want to cooperate after all. After a few days of feeding her up and engaging her in sensible talks, I sent her back to her mother.

The next time I rang them up and asked after Keeley, she lived on the streets again.

'I couldn't hold her,' was her mother's excuse.

Hopeless woman, my daughter, I thought. What Keeley needs is a few boundaries and a lot more attention from a fair but consistent grown-up than she had been getting all her life. Now it was too late.

I saw my grand-daughter again, or rather she saw me, when I did my Christmas shopping. She frightened the life out of me, suddenly sidling up to me in the middle of the pavement.

'Can I come and stay again?' she smirked, as if it was her God given right. There was also a hint of menace in her voice.

'Why would you want to do that?' I asked cautiously. That vicious girl gang could be round the corner for all I knew, just waiting to pounce on me and snatch my handbag with my Christmas money.

'I think I had enough,' she said and looked as if she meant it.

What possessed me to believe her and to take her in again, I don't know. Maybe I still saw somewhere in her the girl I had wanted her to be. Hope springs eternal, I suppose.

No sooner had we settled down to a cup of tea and had sorted out where she was going to sleep, the police knocked on the door. Something about beating up another girl the previous Friday night outside a disco.

I don't know what shocked me more: that she had participated in assaulting another human being or her excuse, which she thought might mitigate the circumstances, that she was blind drunk. A girl of her age? At that time of night, she should have been tucked up in bed with her teddy bear.

She was put on bail but her mother didn't want to know anymore. So Keeley stayed with me again.

Right, I thought, this will give me a chance to inject some order into my grand-daughter's messed-up life.

At first she enjoyed our chats and sounded quite reasonable. I even managed to enrol her again in the school down the road. Of course, I expected to hear from them soon, but to my surprise, I didn't.

Keeley also seemed to enjoy the little tasks I gave her like feeding the cat, or mowing the grass of my tiny garden and pruning the shrubs. A bit of responsibility might bring her out, I thought.

And it did – at first. I didn't even mind giving her a modest amount of pocket money when she asked but I kept a vigilant eye on my savings tin at the back in one of the kitchen cupboards, just in case. Once she bought me a pot of pathetically weak violets with her money. Goodness knows where she got it from; definitely something a florist would want to get rid of but the thought was nice and I gave her a hug and praised her for her thoughtfulness. She seemed to lap it up.

I thought we had grown pretty close, but I drew the line at calling her KIP; I was not one of her friends; to me she would always be Keeley.

As it was half-term holidays, I organised a little job for her in the local newsagents, only three hours to start with, to be extended if she wanted to, but on day three I had a call from the shopkeeper asking why she hadn't turned up.

She did turn up for lunch, pretending that she had worked overtime, but realised looking at my stony face that instead of being impressed I was mad with her.

'Why didn't you just say that it wasn't for you?'

I had my suspicions that it wasn't the type of work she didn't like, it was work in general she objected to. She hung her head when I gave my little lecture on the advantages of going to work and impressed upon her that this was the only way to pull herself out of her situation and move onwards and upwards.

I really warmed to my theme and argued more passionately than I had ever done in my life. It felt as if she was standing on a cliff and I tried to save her from jumping off.

She did go back to the shop for another day, but at the weekend she was suddenly gone with her few belongings and the contents of my savings tin. No note, no good-bye, nothing. As it turned out, she had helped herself to money from the shop's till as well.

The next thing I knew, I was called as a character witness. Keeley had gone back to the girl gang, and now they were all in front of the Court for assault, criminal damage, theft and shoplifting.

'Do I have to?' I asked the community policewoman. 'I really don't' want anything to do with her anymore. It's so upsetting!'

'I am sorry,' he said, 'I do understand,' but I still had to go and tell them all about her.

I told it truthfully; I don't know any other way. It made me feel sad, not vengeful. I was getting to an age where I needed my peace and quiet, and the problems of the young generation had a habit of getting rather on top of me. I just wanted to be left alone.

I was just turning round to climb down from the witness stand, when a clear, familiar voice shouted: 'You old slag. I knew I couldn't count on you! Eff-off out of my life!'

I was so shocked that I tripped on the step and would have fallen, had not a nice young woman in a wig grabbed my elbow and steadied me – quite something considering my weight!

Keeley was convicted and given some sort of pathetic sentence, probably suspended. Thankfully, I heard nothing further …

Until today.

'So what are your plans?'

'Can I stay, Gran?'

'No.' I am adamant and my voice is firm. I really don't want to be dragged into problems anymore. I am too old.

She begins to cry. I give her a tissue to wipe her eyes and blow her nose.

'Tell me what happened since I saw you last,' I ask. I do feel sorry for her, but she has brought it upon herself really.

I lean forward and she begins:

'They sent me to a young offenders' institution, only for a month. For the rest of my sentence I did community service, helping the down and outs… I actually quite liked that,' she muses and nibbles at her lower lip. She is still sitting on my sofa in the same crouched position, this horrible, black cloak covering her like a tent.

I stay quiet; it's up to her to tell me more. I am at least willing to listen which is probably more than other people would do.

'Just after I was released I met Ahmed in a caff, where I was working the morning shift. Ahmed is a taxi driver; he sometimes has breakfast there. He loves English breakfast, but his family mustn't know because they are Muslims and Muslims are not allowed to eat pork. I thought that was great, him defying his parents.'

Yes, I can see why that would impress her: defying authority was always Keeley's speciality.

'He invited me out for a coke; then he took me to the movies. I really wanted him to take me to a disco or a night club, but he wouldn't, and he made it clear that if I wanted to be his girlfriend he didn't want me to go to these place.'

Aha, the first person to set those famous boundaries. Why does it work with total strangers and not with her own mother?

'How old is he?' and I am surprised when she says 'twenty-one'. So disciplined at twenty-one, but that's probably how he has been brought up.

'He also doesn't believe in sex before marriage,' she blurts out, 'which was a real problem. The times we nearly got carried away. Just kissing was already a sin in his religion.' She almost giggles now.

Do I want to know all this? But I can't help comparing that in my youth it was exactly like that; none of this getting drunk and getting laid by the first bloke who showed an interest. We saved ourselves, as my mother put it. You saved yourself for your husband if you could somehow manage it. Not everybody did of course, but at least one tried.

'Go on,' I encourage her.

'Well, he introduced me to his parents who weren't too keen, but accepted me when Ahmed told them that we wanted to get married. They arranged it all. Of course, most of his family are back in Bangladesh, so it was a small wedding. We got married in the registry office and then his parents organised a Muslim celebration. They bought me a *sari* and some jewellery, and then someone came from their mosque and married us again. Afterwards there was tea and special biscuits and the family put on some Bengali music and we all hopped around the living room; not his parents, but us young ones.'

'That was nice,' I say unenthusiastically. It doesn't seem to me the stuff that dreams are made of.

There was no stopping her now, as she burbled on:

'At first, I quite liked it, the daily routine, getting up, my husband going to work, me in the kitchen with his mum preparing his dinner. I wasn't too keen on praying five times a day – I usually skipped the morning one – but I did most of it. Well, I just did the gestures and pretended; I had no idea what his mother was saying, it was all in their language, but I said a little prayer I had learnt in nursery school.

'So what went wrong?' I barge in to hurry her up. I want her gone before my friend Phil comes.

'We had taken a few days off as a sort of honeymoon. We mainly stayed in our room, in bed.'

I cringe but don't say a word.

'When Ahmed went back to work he cancelled my job in the caff without asking me first. I went spare. He explained that as his wife I didn't need to go out to work. I put up a fight and said, I wanted to, but he said that now I belonged to him and he wouldn't allow me; it would reflect badly on him and the family if he let me work there, men coming in and all that. Something else then, I said, but he wouldn't hear of it…and by the way, he said, I want you to wear our clothes. You are a Muslim wife and you have to dress modestly.'

She sits there as if she can't believe her own words.

I can well imagine the scene. She must have felt like an animal on which the cage doors clattered shut one by one.

'He told me to learn Bengali recipes from his mother, and from then on I did nothing but housework and cooking. I was so bored I tried to talk to her but she hardly speaks English. She is perfectly happy with her life; but it's not enough for me. This is not what I wanted!'

What can I say? It's ironical, really: The wildest girl in town falls under the spell of a strict Muslim husband.

'Have you told him?' I ask.

She is cagey: 'He is never there, and I don't think he is always working when he says he is. But when I question him he has all sorts of excuses – someone has to earn money, is a favourite – and when I dig deeper, he gets angry…'

I wonder how angry.

She pauses, takes a deep breath and continues: 'After about three months, I had enough and I slipped out – I wasn't really allowed out without his mother or father – and asked in the nursery down the road whether they needed an assistant. Nobody could object to that, surely, but Ahmed was furious. He was beside himself and accused me of defying him. And then he…' She can hardly get herself to utter the words: 'He hit me… in the face.'

'Why didn't you run away?' I ask, wanting to add 'as you usually did', but I bite my tongue. Now is not the time to be sarcastic.

She begins to sob again, her body convulsed with sorrow.

'What did his parents say?' I enquire to bridge the gap and to jump-start the conversation again.

She takes another paper tissue from the rapidly emptying box and blows her nose noisily.

'Nothing. They pretend they haven't heard anything. To them it hasn't happened.'

'Then he found out that I had a criminal record. Don't ask me how; I hadn't told him. He probably opened one of my letters from the Social Services. From then on, I wasn't allowed out anywhere, not with him, not with his parents. I wasn't even allowed to make phone calls.'

It is too dreadful. No one deserves to be treated like this. I try again: 'Would you like a cup of tea now?' She nods. I go to my kitchen; it gives me time to think. I boil the kettle and let the teabag mash to brew a strong cuppa.

'Still milk and two sugars?' I shout through the open door and I hear: 'Yes, please,' surprised that I remembered.

'So what happened next?'

I shudder to think.

'My periods stopped.'

Oh, God!

'His mother bought me a pregnancy test and it was positive. Ahmed was shocked. 'Shit!' he said, but when his father congratulated him, he felt quite proud and manly. That night he totally forgot himself; he felt all-powerful. I told him that he hurt me but he didn't listen, or maybe he didn't care.'

'Soon afterwards, I over-heard a conversation he had with some mates who had come to the house. I was shut in our bedroom because I wasn't to show my face: it was .indecent, he said. But I could still hear him bragging at the top of his voice, that now that he was going to be the father of a child born in England and to a British mother, his problems were over. He and his parents would no longer be illegal immigrants. Instead they would soon be the proud owners of British passports. He sounded totally confident… So now I knew: He had married me to stay in the country.' Sobs resurface and her voice filled with bitterness and disappointment.

'When his mates left, I confronted him. I wasn't going to

take this lying down. His parents knew something was up and withdrew to the kitchen. This time he did not only slap me round the face, he beat me up.'

Keeley lifts that horrible black garment off her arms and legs and shows me her bruises.

'I have more all over my body.'

I believe her.

'How did you get out today to come here?'

'I nicked his mother's keys when she had an afternoon nap; Ahmed and his father are at work. I slipped out quietly.'

That's new; she used to slam doors when exiting.

I still haven't made up my mind whether I shall let her stay with me. The more I hear, the more I think that I haven't got a choice. My heart is not made of stone. She is so young; she has gone through so much, not all of it her own fault. If her mother had given her more attention; if the teachers hadn't been so overstretched and had simply chucked her out... She is a good girl really, my Keeley!

Or am I kidding myself?

I decide: There is no harm in giving her another chance... second, third or fourth, what does it matter?

I am ripped out of my thoughts by the doorbell. Keeley's eyes fill with fear.

'That will be my friend Phil,' I say for reassurance.

I have gone all rigid with sitting so long, but I manage to heave myself up and shuffle to the door.

'Who is it?' I call out as I always do. 'Phil, is that you?'

Although I don't get an answer, I open it, leaving the chain on as a precaution.

I can see through the gap that it is not Phil but a dark-skinned boy whose brown eyes are burning into my face.

'Is Asha there?'

'Who?' I am genuinely baffled.

'Asha!'

I dig in my heels. No boyo, I am not going to react until you call her by the name her mother gave her!

'Keeley,' he spits out finally as if clearing his throat.

'She is called Asha now... it means *light*.' As if that makes it any better. Through how many names is this girl going? Keeley Isla, Kip and now Asha...

'Is she here?' I can see from his fidgeting and blazing eyes that he is getting impatient.

I don't answer his question.

'Who are you?' I demand.

'Her husband,' he draws himself up to his full height, as if he was her guardian.

'Right', I say to win time. I must defend her, keep her safe.

And then something strange happens: I hear a swishing of cloth and can feel it brush past me.

'I was just coming, Ahmed,' my grand-daughter of many names says sweetly, unhooks the chain and opens the door wide. I nearly drop dead. What if he attacks us?

She even attempts a little smile.

'I only came to tell my grandmother that we are expecting a baby,' she trills apologetically, ducking a little as if expecting a blow.

When it doesn't come she carries on, smothering him with words: 'I know I should have told you in advance but I forgot. You don't mind, do you? You know I like to keep in contact with my family.' She is almost breathless now.

You could blow me down with a feather. I look at him. She has obviously taken the wind out of his angry sails.

'Good!' he says with irritation and is already turning to go down the stairway, expecting her to follow.

'Can I come again?' she whispers when he is out of earshot. 'I mean when the baby is born?'

'My great-grand-child, eh?' I can't help feeling a flicker of affection for this innocent little mite.

'You are sure you don't want to stay?' I plead. She is too young to suffer from 'battered wife syndrome'.

She shakes her head slowly as if in a trance:

'Better not. It's easier that way.'

'Take care.' I say, 'you know where to find me.'

She gives me a hug and rushes after her young husband.

'Byeeee!' she shouts, already halfway down the stairs.

'Bye.' The word almost gets stuck in my throat.

I hear a few voices below by the entrance door, one party going out and another trying to come in. This must be Phil. I hear her puffing up the stairs.

'Those stairs will one day be the death of us,' she greets me.

'Nice young couple. Were they with you?' she asks distractedly, peering with interest at the empty mug.

'Yes, my grand-daughter and her husband. They came unexpectedly... to tell me that they are having a baby.'

'Lovely,' Phil says, already having lost interest. There comes a time when old people have to let the young get on with their own lives.

Maybe I should?

'I go and make us a cup of tea,' I say.

'Yes, and I won a bit of money at Bingo, so I bought us a doughnut each,' she licks her lips and begins to rummage round her plastic shopping bag.

Again, I go to the kitchen, shaking my head. I am exhausted, And wonder whether I have done the right thing, letting her go. At least she knows now that she can always find shelter with me, my KIP. I smile and fill the kettle.

CASEY

CASEY

My friend Celia twists her handkerchief with trembling hands. Her big, blue eyes are staring at a tiny dot in the distance, willing it to hurry along the farm track towards us. I squeeze her plump hand in solidarity.

We stand outside the modest Alabama farm house which has been home to Celia and Bill for all their married life.

She stretches her stout body to its full height which sets off the thick red curls framing her round face like yoyos. She glances furtively back to where Bill, her husband of forty years, paces up and down the wooden veranda, occasionally bumping into the bird feeders tied to the beams.

'You look great,' I call over to him and can't help smiling. I have never seen him dressed up like this, in brand new jeans and a fresh blue and white checked flannel shirt which brings out the colour of his eyes.

He has even washed his usually greasy mop of grey hair and every now and then pats down the still wet, unruly strands.

¤ ¤ ¤ ¤ ¤

There is a fading wedding photograph on their sitting room wall bearing witness to the moment when they had got married as teenage sweethearts. Bill had worn a white shirt with an enormous collar, flared black trousers and his best cowboy boots while Celia had resembled a three-tiered wedding cake in her ample taffeta and tulle creation, which had been the fashion of that time. Both are smiling deliriously happy into the camera.

They had grown up in the small world of an Alabama farming community and had always known what was 'the done thing' and what was not. Marrying young was fine, marrying outside their circle would not have been acceptable. During all their years of marriage, they had lived by their parents' code of morals and values and had handed them down once their daughter Patricia was born.

However, when Patricia had grown into a teenager, she had soon shown tendencies of not wanting to conform and of being bored with the life her parents led.

'Where are you going?' Celia would ask and the only answer she would get was: 'Out!'

Patricia was certainly not as malleable as they had been. It was a great disappointment to them.

By the time, she was sixteen she was slipping out of their grip. They never knew where she was going or whether she was telling the truth, until one day Bill took down the bull whip. Patricia left the farm there and then.

They were hoping against hope to hear on the grapevine that she had escaped to further studies at college or even university. They would have rushed to her side and been supportive, but they were horrified at what they did hear: a squalid squat in the state capital and a life of booze, drugs and – they suspected – prostitution.

They hadn't heard from Patricia for several years, when she suddenly turned up at their doorstep with a toddler in tow. She looked ill, hollow cheeked, grey skin, deep black circles under her sunken eyes, the lids of which were at constant half-mast.

'That's Casey,' she mumbled pointing vaguely at the little girl who was clinging on to her mother's hand. Patricia freed herself with a jerk and kept her arms out of reach of the tiny palms which were struggling to get a limpet-like grip again.

There were questions written all over her parents' faces.

'She is three years old,' Patricia spluttered incoherently and with defiance.

'Honey, would you like…'

Bill waved angrily at his wife to be quiet.

'Now young lady, let me tell you…'

Before he could finish the sentence, Patricia had turned round and tottered away on her high heels along the farm track, battling against her tight pencil skirt and unzipped black leather jacket.

The little girl stood there as if frozen to the spot, watching her mother disappearing from her life.

'You want a lift somewhere?' Bill cleared his throat to get the words out. 'It's a long way to the bus stop…' He had to shout even louder as his daughter had nearly reached the gate at the end of the track.

Patricia did not turn around as her wavering figure got smaller and smaller.

Bill shrugged his shoulders, peered at the little girl looking up at him with fear in her eyes.

'Welcome, Casey,' he said gruffly before turning away to attend to his cattle.

'Come with me, Casey. You must be parched,' Celia took charge of her grand-daughter, who, eyes to the ground, followed her like a little dog.

¤ ¤ ¤ ¤ ¤

From that moment on, Casey embarked on an idyllic country childhood. She helped her grandmother with planting vegetables and feeding the chickens. As she grew older her grandfather roped her in to look after the cattle and the horses.

For her eighth birthday she was given her own horse, a black mare called Ebony who was gentle and obedient. Casey got up early every morning before school to muck out and feed her and never once did she miss the school bus home because she knew that Ebony was waiting by the fence to go out for a ride.

Casey was an easy child to bring up – unlike her mother – a little insecure perhaps which, considering her past, was no surprise but she was always willing to please, willing to be helpful; she never once complained.

'Casey, could you…?' Usually they had hardly finished the request when she would come running.

She showed little interest in a life outside, refusing most invitations with the excuse that she had things to do on the farm. Where the grandparents had expected battles, there were none.

She wasn't the prettiest of girls, but nobody in their farming community judged people by their looks. It was the mucking in, helping out and a sunny disposition that counted – and Casey had plenty of that!

Casey was loved, cherished and encouraged to study and to achieve. During examination time, her grandparents took over all responsibilities on the farm, so that she could prepare without disturbances.

To everyone's delight, she proved to be clever and sailed through school exams with ease. She loved reading and writing little stories – usually about animals – which were at first read out in assemblies at school and later published in the parish magazine until the local newspaper got hold of one and printed it, too.

During her last year at school, Casey mentioned that her

French teacher was looking for host families for a group of European exchange students. Casey would have loved to have someone her own age stay with them for a week, but she knew that there wasn't any spare money to send her on the return visit to France.

'The school has a fund to pay for you,' her teacher assured her, 'you are such a good student, you deserve help!'

Casey was so breathlessly excited that her grandparents could hardly refuse.

Celine was the most delightful and exotic guest they had ever had on the farm. She looked so pretty with her long, blond hair falling down her back or, as she did when they went on excursions with the school, piling it elegantly up on her head letting little ringlets escape and fall along her temples.

Casey felt a little dowdy beside her new friend, this heavenly creature from across the Atlantic. Even on the farm Celine managed to look sophisticated, dressed in jeans and a white shirt, the back of its collar standing up emphasising her swanlike neck. In the evenings, she often threw a scarf or pashmina around her slim shoulders and draped it effortlessly to look stunning. To Casey's surprise, Celine did not use much make-up but took great care to clean and nourish her skin. Casey took note.

'No need for tears. I shall see you in three weeks' time in France.' They hugged each other before Celine climbed into the coach which took the group to the airport.

'We get a postcard almost every day,' Celia reported proudly to the neighbours.

'Having a FANTASTIC time!!!' or

'Weather glorious! People sooooooo friendly!'

'Going out with Celine and family to have another adventure!' signing with 'Au revoir' or 'À bientôt!'

71

'Isn't it great!' said her grandparents to each other. They were happy for her to have these new experiences which were beyond their imagination.

What they had not banked on was that Casey would fall in love in France. Neither Celine nor Casey had ever mentioned a brother but when she came home, she could hardly hide the daily long-distance calls, e-mails and pink enveloped letters she sent off.

'Who is that with you and Celine?' Celia probed pointing at the picture on Casey's desk.

'That's Ahmed, Celine's brother.' According to this picture, the teenager was stocky, dark-skinned with fiery eyes, an engaging smile, a flat nose and thick black hair parted neatly on one side.

'He doesn't look anything like her,' her grandmother frowned trying to make sense of it.

'He is adopted. He comes from Algeria.'

Celia didn't quite know how to handle this news and thought it wise to keep it from Bill, until one day he found out for himself.

'I am not having this!' he hissed at Celia when the girl was out of ear shot.

'Please, don't say anything,' Celia begged. 'I couldn't bear...' she began to sob.

After months of furious correspondence, Casey announced: 'Celine and Ahmed would like to come over for their summer holidays.'

They declined and made it clear that they could not afford to send their grand-daughter to France a second time even though she was invited back.

'How am I going to tell them?' How embarrassing is that!' It was the first time that Casey sulked in opposition.

Their refusal had eventually the desired effect, and the friendship having threatened for a while to turn into an infatuation, fizzled out.

The not so desired effect was that Casey continued to be remote and stopped being the loving, trusting girl they had known. Any enquiries into her private life were politely stalled.

'How is school?' They could foretell that everything would be 'fine'.

'Have you heard from Celine?'

'Nope.'

Whenever they were looking for her, they found her with Ebony and had the feeling that she told the horse more than them.

'Teenagers!' they shook their heads and thought no more about it. At least Casey's French marks had improved.

◻ ◻ ◻ ◻ ◻

It was self-understood that Casey would go on to further education. At first she enrolled at the local college to become a student nurse. After a year and a half they were all secretly relieved when she was accepted at another institution, two hours flight from their county airport, to embark on highly specialised nursing qualification.

'Marvellous,' the grandparents thought and were proud. The black cloud of resentment lifted or, at least, moved with their grand-daughter, and the three of them fell into a routine of civilised telephone conversations about her progress.

After a while, they lost track how long her training was supposed to last.

'When will you come back?' they enquired, 'you are bound to get a job at the local hospital,' they assured her and smiled at each other. What an asset she would be to their community!

Ahmed was a far distant memory.

'I won't,' she said to their surprise and with assertiveness, unusual for her.

'I shall finish in summer and I have been offered a job at University Hospital as a nurse in the operating theatre.'

She must have done well being head-hunted for such a job, and the two elderly people on their farm understood that she couldn't turn down such an opportunity.

However, they missed her, and Ebony rested her head every afternoon on the fence looking forlornly whether her mistress would get off the school bus this time.

They had often wondered what Casey's social life was like, but they didn't want to pry and she didn't ever give anything away, not even during her brief visit at Christmas. She was chattier than they remembered her, had let her hair grow and put it up neatly in a bun, like Celine had done, and was dressed demurely, in an old-fashioned, chic way.

After that visit, the telephone calls became sporadic.

'She is probably too busy with her new job,' they consoled themselves.

Then one sticky, hot Sunday afternoon, at the height of the Alabama summer, she dropped a bombshell into their rural idyll: 'I would like you to come to my wedding,' she said, determination and apprehension clearly wrestling for her vocal cords.

'Casey, Honey, what a surprise! Who is it?' Celia gushed.

'Well,' it was a long drawn-out syllable,' he is a doctor at the University Hospital; he also teaches at the college and he is lovely, and, more to the point, he loves me!' She sounded so happy.

'What's his name?' It was just a throw-away question; the answer wasn't really important, but they had better know what to call him.

'Ahmed.' They were bewildered. That wasn't a common American name. 'What sort of name is that?' they asked still joyous and oblivious to the hornets' nest.

'He is from Algeria.'

'Algeria? It's not…?'

'Yes, it is Celine's brother.'

A painful silence ensued on both sides as they realised that they, the only relatives she had, would not be attending her wedding.

The receivers at either end of the line were put back stiffly into their cradles.

'A coloured man!' Bill spat on the floor, something he hadn't done since he had been a youngster; he remembered, it had earned him a clip around the ear from his father.

¤ ¤ ¤ ¤ ¤

For years, bitterness clouded the memories of their grand-daughter's childhood. Celia often sobbed secretly while her husband stomped grumpily around the farm.

'Why am I working my fingers to the bone?' he would complain, 'and for whom?' a question which would remain hanging in the air, because Celia couldn't think of the answer either.

For a second time, they had failed and lost a daughter; for a second time, all the love, support and care they had so freely given, had been thrown back into their faces. Marrying outside their circle, a foreigner and worst of all, a coloured man, did not fit into their age-old code of morals, values and expectations. They were devastated. They never mentioned her name, not between each other nor to friends. Neighbours and people in their community soon stopped asking about Casey, fearing that the answer would be short and brusque.

¤ ¤ ¤ ¤ ¤

I met Celia during those difficult years, and we developed a friendship in spite of my blatantly tolerant and liberal attitudes and my oriental looking husband.

I was a teacher at the local elementary school and had roped Celia in as a parent governor. She came two days a week to help with pupils who had trouble with reading. She learnt to love all the children, whatever their background, and soon felt at ease with them.

'Can marriages between coloured and white people work?' she asked one evening, when I had invited her to my home and we were both a little tipsy.

I burst out laughing: 'Look at me and Nurul. We have been married five hundred years; at least, it feels like that.'

Celia nodded, remaining serious.

'Do you mind if I ask you silly questions like that?' she hiccupped.

'Of course not!' I hugged her.

We liked each other, and that was all that counted.

Swallowing hard, she told me Casey's story.

'I wish, Bill would change his mind,' she ended, 'so I could feel free to contact her.'

'It will happen,' I consoled her and hoped fervently that I was right.

¤   ¤   ¤   ¤   ¤

A few weeks later, we sat at her kitchen table having coffee when the telephone rang.

'Hi,' she fiddled distractedly with the twisted cord, and then nearly stumbled with shock. I pushed a chair towards her and indicated that she should sit down.

'It's Casey, Grandma. I just wanted you to know that you have a great-grand-daughter. We called her Celia Celine.' I could hear the words tumbling like a waterfall.

My friend Celia began to sob with happiness.

'Are you alright?' Casey's voice trembled with concern, so I took the phone and told her that her grandmother, the only mother she had ever known, was weeping with happiness.

'Do you really think so?' Casey sounded touchingly hopeful.

'Yes, I don't only think so, I know so; I am her best friend!'

At that moment, Celia senior wrestled the receiver back and said, her voice almost flipping over with emotion:

'You must come and see us soon!' adding a pleading, 'please!'

Relieved and surprised laughter came from the other end.

'Well, I had hoped for an invitation, but I must warn you, I shall bring all three of us, Ahmed included!'

'He will be most welcome!' Celia raised herself to her full height with a new dignity which would leave her husband no choice but to accept her decision.

¤　¤　¤　¤　¤

'Here they come!' Celia jumps up and down in front of the veranda.

I can hear the humming birds behind us at the feeders, beating their wings furiously as if they were part of the excitement.

Bill stands next to his wife, grinning sheepishly at her youthful exuberance. A big white car, glinting in the bright sunlight, crawls along the farm track to reunite the family.

TRACEY

TRACEY

Kasim was in a dilemma. He was in love – unfortunately not with the woman his parents had in mind for him. Had they known about his dalliance they would have been horrified and made it clear that he was in love with the wrong woman.

He loved Tracey, with her soft, plump body; her heavy breasts squeezed into tight tops, almost spilling out; her bleached blond locks; her wide hips, promising for child bearing (but probably not for his child); her big blue eyes standing a little too wide apart in her round face, her retroussé nose and the fullness of her mouth. He often compared her lips to plumped up cushions and found them eminently kissable. Her smile brought a grin to his face as it revealed a big gap between her front teeth; it made her look like a little girl.

She had an easy-going manner confident, stern when required but immensely practical, sensible and unflappable as only a nurse could be. When he had first met her, she had assured him that she loved nothing better than her job. This suited him fine, but as their relationship had flourished into a full blown affair, she had hinted more than once that she would not be averse to giving marriage and motherhood priority. He had hardly listened, burying his head happily between her breasts or drowning himself in the folds around her belly button and the sweet smell of her unblemished, rosy skin.

Her murmurings grew stronger, louder, more demanding. He still ignored them, brushing them aside with embarrassed jollity and spontaneous embraces. Most times he succeeded in diverting her, making her question in her own mind whether they should just continue to be happy the way they were; whether she was asking too much; whether she was pushing him too fast; and finally, whether they needed formalisation of any kind at all.

She tried to convince herself that she had every reason to feel secure in his love and fought hard against the nagging doubts which kept popping up in her head: Would he ever commit? More to the point, could he ever commit? He had rarely spoken about his family in Bangladesh, never mind introduced her to any friends or relatives living in England. He wasn't even keen to be introduced to her circle of friends or her family.

There was only one couple they had been out with once or twice, a woman much older than her Bengali boyfriend who was in his third year at a London University college.

'He'll have to return to Bangladesh once his course is finished,' Kasim declared gloomily. As he hadn't looked at Tracey uttering those words of doom for that particular relationship, she deduced that theirs was quite of a different kind, and that the chances of its survival were much better.

Whenever Kasim received letters from home, he would be subdued and deep in thought for the rest of the weekend, the only time they could really meet up. She was then left with worry for a whole week whilst in her room at the nurses' wing or rushing around hospital corridors during shifts. Could those letters from his country ever take him away from her? She had no idea whether the world they came from had any such influence or power. Sometimes he spoke about his childhood, this place or another he had known or played in. It sounded exotic, far away and vastly different to her own upbringing in the East End of London.

'Have you ever mentioned me to your parents?' she asked tentatively when Kasim was in a particularly good mood.

'Of course not,' was his guarded reply. This baffled her but as she didn't want to spoil their time of togetherness and love-making she didn't dig any further.

The months passed and, convinced that her hold on his love grew stronger every week, she voiced more enquiries as to where their relationship was going. Kasim became prickly and sheepish and didn't ring her as often on weekday evenings. He also excused himself from joining her at the weekend with a fairly plausible explanation, concerning some sort of family celebration of a far distant cousin.

'Can't I come?' she asked disappointment about a rejection already in her voice. She knew the answer before he came out with it.

'Look, this is Bengali society. I can't introduce you unless we are married.' She looked up at him hopefully, but he wouldn't be drawn whether that was on the cards. She would have to be content with meeting him again in a fortnight.

There followed a few weeks where she had to work nights and weekends, and they found it hard to meet up at all. Kasim ran, as far as she knew, a company on behalf of a relative and professed having to work hard to prove himself. What exactly that consisted of, he never said, but he must have been doing well, because he lived in a huge house. At first, she had thought that it was far too big for one person, but he had explained that it actually belonged to his parents and that the family used it as a home from home on their annual visits.

The house was situated in an affluent area of West London, he drove a flashy sports car, only dressed in designer labelled clothes and took her out to expensive restaurants, which she couldn't have afforded; he also gave her thoughtful and expensive presents like perfumes, jewellery, weekends away with him – everything she had ever desired, except for the ring.

It wasn't the wealth which attracted her; yes, it was nice and made life comfortable, but ultimately it wasn't her money. She hadn't just been swept off her feet by Kasim, she really loved him and she certainly didn't want to lose him. Her only option was therefore, to be patient. In her mind, she could see herself keeping house, doing the occasional agency nursing stint until she would expect his lovely, olive-skinned baby. She loved to daydream about it and had sometimes to be called back to reality by a demanding patient.

¤ ¤ ¤ ¤ ¤

Kasim had not been entirely right about the odd couple, the older Italian woman and the young Bengali student. The latter had recently finished his university course and, instead of returning home and each going their separate ways, they had decided to get married, so that he could stay in the country while they chose where ultimately they wanted to live.

It was the first occasion to which Kasim and Tracey were invited together as a couple. The wedding was a small, registry office affair, as either parents of the bride and groom could not or would not attend. There were only a handful of guests, friends and a supportive Italian aunt who had refused to miss her niece's big day. She was a real live-wire and created a lot of jollity with her exuberance: 'It is your lucky day!' she proclaimed vociferously several times, and all in all it turned out to be a happy day.

Tracey had made every effort to look elegant in her ice-blue sleeveless dress with a scalloped décolleté just showing a little bit of her ample cleavage. For modesty, she had covered up her fleshy arms with a navy chiffon shawl. The look was completed by stylish high-heeled shoes and some of Kasim's jewellery, just enough to remain within the boundaries of good taste. More than ever she longed to put something on her wedding ring finger.

Maybe the happy couple's obvious joy in each other and the general atmosphere of love and hope in a joint future might bring something on in Kasim's mind, but as he dropped her back at the nurses' accommodation, he gave her a passionate kiss and explained that he would be away for a couple of weeks, mainly on business.

She usually knew these things in advance, but this time he had sprung it on her. And it wasn't just for a few days but the vague amount of a couple of weeks.

During all that time away, she had one hasty phone call from his mobile:

'Where are you?' she asked anxiously twiddling a lock of her hair.

'So far I was on business in Sri Lanka. Being so close, I decided to pop in on my folks,' he said as if he had to whisper in a far corner of the hotel.

She wasn't entirely sure how far Sri Lanka and Bangladesh were from each other but it didn't look close on the map in her world atlas.

'That's nice,' she said unconvincingly. She would have loved to have been there, too!

'When will you be back?' she continued with trepidation?

'Probably in a week. There is a family wedding coming up which is always an elaborate affair, so I might as well take a few days extra leave and do my filial duty.'

At least another week! Tracey almost burst into tears. There was no point in asking whether she could join him. It would only embarrass or anger him; after all, they still weren't married. And to be honest, she didn't think that she would be given time off from the hospital at such short notice.

She would spend the weekend with her family in the East End of London.

◻   ◻   ◻   ◻   ◻

'I am being a rat!' Kasim confided in a younger member of his family. 'I really do love that English girl!'

'You can't disappoint and disobey your parents; they would be heart-broken!' was the advice which settled the matter once and for all.

His parents had no idea that he had an English girlfriend and would approve even less if he married her. He had racked his brain for a solution, a way around the problem. He was sure that he would have had a wonderfully uncomplicated life with Tracey – not many demands, a lot of love and fun, an easy-going and passionate relationship with the odd ups and downs, but generally lovely and predictable, the world open to both of them.

It was a dream, an unfeasible dream, and he knew it. Tracey would just have to find somebody else to be happy with. English girls usually moved on quite quickly…

This last thought hurt.

It was expected of him to marry a Bengali girl of equal standing: well educated, from a good family and above all, untarnished; in return he hoped for a little of Tracey's prettiness and voluptuousness.

He was at a loss what he would do about Tracey herself, once he would have returned to London with his bride. It would come to him, he was sure. In a way, she had probably known all along that he was never going to marry her.

Slipping his mobile into the pocket of his white pyjama trousers, he tugged nervously on the richly embroidered and beaded sleeve of his Sherwani jacket. He had refused to admire himself in the mirror knowing that he would not have recognised himself in this outfit.

A little sad but determined, he turned to plunge himself headlong into the festivities of his own wedding.

¤   ¤   ¤   ¤   ¤

He was delighted with the joy he seemed to spread around the two families by simply complying with their wishes. His new wife wasn't bad at all – a clever girl with glasses and a university degree; long, straight, black hair falling down to her tiny waist; a little skinny, perhaps, but this would change after a child or two;

after all she was only twenty-two years of age. So far she had been shy with him but that was to be expected. She had had a sheltered upbringing, no boyfriend to date, his family had been promised; and his parents in turn had proclaimed unkowingly and with a good conscience that their son was a virgin, too.

The young couple would spend their honeymoon in India, somewhere around the Taj Mahal from where they would fly to England to begin their new, married life.

The honeymoon wasn't entirely successful due to his young wife having a tendency to feel faint in the searing heat, having to retire to their hotel suite frequently.

Sitting there on his own in the heavenly gardens of this monument of eternal love, Kasim suddenly missed Tracey. If she were here, she wouldn't feel faint; they would have a wonderful time. He suddenly longed for her soft embrace, her easy laughter, her endless understanding, her unquestioning loyalty; he longed for her like a man longs for water in a desert.

Without much ado, he changed his wife's flight, sending her back to her parents under the pretext that he needed to spruce up the house in London for her benefit. She would now fly from Dhaka in three weeks' time while he would be busy preparing her arrival waiting eagerly and in great anticipation.

In truth he rushed straight from the airport to Tracey's room and they made passionate love over and over again. It felt so natural, so true and right, and they were so terribly happy.

Kasim did not get round to refurbishing his house during those last delicious weeks of freedom. He almost forgot that he was a married man. He certainly did not have the heart to tell Tracey now. He would do so later.

They spent nearly every free minute together; she even took a few days' leave. She was convinced that now he would pop the question.

87

The date of his wife's arrival appeared all too soon and pierced Karim's fog of ecstasy.

Tracey still had no idea; she would have to go back to work tomorrow.

That fateful morning, Karim kissed her passionately good-bye and just left as if going to work.

There was no key for his house to be re-called; she never had one. He closed the door softly with a heavy heart, knowing that his bachelorhood was well and truly over.

Tracey would cry her eyes out, but it couldn't be helped.

ZIO

ZIO

I love my uncle Gino and his wife, auntie Phyllis, the sister
of my late father. In spite of their age, they are still like turtle
doves. She is delicately pretty and hasn't lost her English rose
complexion; she dresses daily with great care and conservative
elegance and winds her long, white hair artfully into a ballerina
chignon in the nape of her neck. If complimented she will joke:
'I have to compete with all the stylish women in his country,' to
which he, her husband of sixty years, will smile indulgently like
a proud father would smile at the peccadillos of his teenage
daughter.

Zio Gino's appearance contrasts starkly with that of his willowy
wife: He is stocky, prone to a rotund waist which gives rise to the
only rows they ever have. Every so often, she tries to put him
on a diet – for his own good, as she assures him. I have seen
photos when he was a young man, boasting his athletic physique
to the camera, clad only in swimming trunks on a sandy beach,
the turquoise Mediterranean sea in the background, sparkling
under a deep blue sky. Just before taking the photograph, he
must have been swimming because his tanned skin glistened
in the sun; a gold chain reflected so strongly in the light as if
it had burnt a hole into his chest. Even in this old photograph,
his thick, black hair, blazing eyes and impeccably white teeth
revealed by a big grin make him look enormously seductive. I
can quite understand why auntie Phyllis fell for him.

His hair has thinned and I am not sure whether his teeth are
still all his own but his southern Italian charm has not waned.
Unfortunately, Zio Gino is not very well these days – lung trouble,

my auntie hinted; not surprising, really, after a lifetime of smoking rough cigarettes. When he was young, nobody knew that smoking was bad for health; it made teenagers look cool and feel grown up. As Zio Gino grew older, smoking had become a habit which was difficult to break, partly due to lack of conviction and partly because of his pride that men knew best. Now the body had taken its revenge.

Still, apart from having become portly, his face being criss-crossed by furrows and his breath sometimes coming in bursts of laboured wheezes, he is still the same to me:

'*Chi se vede!* Look who is here! *Mia nipote bellissima!*' he shouts as I enter the room where he sits like a lord in his ancient arm chair. As I bend down, he envelopes me in a bear hug and smothers my cheeks with kisses. He wears tight jeans, a white open-necked shirt and the old gold chain around his neck. I suppress a giggle remembering his warning from years ago – before we set off for a holiday with his family in Italy – that I shouldn't even consider to fall in love with young men in such attire. 'They don't make good husbands,' he used to say, 'In summer they are beach bums and in winter shepherds in the hills.'

'Sit down, cara mia!' And turning to his wife who stands in the doorway, he gesticulates: 'Phyllis, give-a that child something to eat. Look how thin she is!'

It is the same rigmarole every time and we women fall in with it just to keep him amused.

I voice a fake protest assuring him that I am a grown woman, in my mid-thirties, and that I am curvy enough, but they take no notice. My auntie shrugs her shoulders, rushes out to the kitchen and returns with a tray full of cups, saucers, plates and a selection of Italian cakes, which she gets weekly from the delicatessen in town. Their only concession to old age is now coffee produced by a coffee machine rather than boiled on the stove in a metal pot.

'Espresso is not good for his heart,' she explains but he pooh-poohs this with an angry wave of his stubby fingers.

In the evening, he invariably insists on cooking for us his version, the only acceptable one, of pasta Bolognese. This gives me and my aunt the opportunity for a girlie chat. She still loves to discuss fashion, family gossip, the arts, music and books but her most favourite topics are still my affairs of the heart and her memories of their courtship. She can never emphasize enough the big role luck had played in that they had met at all.

¤   ¤   ¤   ¤   ¤

Zio Gino had grown up in the southernmost part of Italy, hot, dusty, poor and largely ignored by the industrial North. Most men earned their living as fishermen, few had the good fortune of learning a trade like car mechanics, bricklaying, plumbing or electrics; very few were known to have gone on to higher education and had moved away to study at university somewhere far away like Rome. Those young people rarely returned.

Zio Gino had been one of the first to seek his fortune abroad.

Further inland, towards the Apennine Mountains were farms, but that, too, was a hard life on the arid, steep, deforested hills under a baking sun with only bony cows, greedy goats and stubborn mules and donkeys for company.

Termoli, my uncle's home town, was a romantic little place, perched on a hill, the old quarters enveloped by a medieval city wall; it only had two openings to the world, an arch for entrance and another for exit. The houses were sturdy, many built into rock and occupied for generations by the same families.

They wanted nothing to do with the people of the 'new town' which over the years had sprung up below. Hotels and their cheaper versions of *albergos*, plus restaurants, *gelaterias* and souvenir shops had grown like mushrooms along the beach and inland to accommodate, feed and amuse tourists.

Goings-on in the 'new town' were disdainfully ignored or watched with suspicion from above.

The house my uncle had grown up in had been one of those which were built into the rock. From the front, it looked identical to all the other ancient town houses: built with local stone, a small entrance door in the middle, tiny windows – to keep the summer's heat out – and a flat roof which was a blessing on sultry evenings because it was shaded by a pergola from which grapes hung in abundance almost into one's mouth. From up there, one could either look down to the *Piazza Duomo*, the church square, and spy on passing neighbours, or, on the other side, admire the dramatic view down a ravine falling into the Adriatic sea. A few thirsty looking trees framed the house on either side. If one attempted to walk round it, the way was blocked by the rock from which it had been hewn.

There were more buildings surrounding the *Piazza*. To the right, the 12th century *Basilica*, home of Saint Basso, protector of seafarers and sea lovers; next to it the priest's rather grand mansion which seemed far too big for him and his pretty house-keeper; and to the left residences of old-established local families, who at times pinned a poster outside on their door when somebody had died.

I had heard people talk about an 11th Century Castle on the outskirts of Termoli but we never went there. From afar, it looked like a gigantic watch-tower.

From the *Piazza*, narrow lanes fanned out between dark buildings, bustling with shoppers and market vendors who offered colourful fresh vegetables, ripe, juicy fruits, placed unceremoniously and without any thought for window dressing on rough wooden planks: and of course, there were smelly tables full of fish, the daily haul of the town's fishermen.

Behind the stalls were the permanent shops of the butcher where huge *salame* and *prosciutto crudo*, salami sausages, and dried Parma hams, hung in the window; *la panetteria*, the baker, offering white loaves and *ciabatta panini*; right next to which was the *pasticceria*, the cake shop; even a *parrucchiere* from whose salon the women all seem to come out with the same permed hairdo; a *generi alimentary:* the grocer, and on the corner, just before the arch in the old city wall, a little office displaying bits and pieces for motorbikes.

Most shop doorways were protected from flies by beaded string curtains which rustled whenever a customer passed through. Overhead, the lanes were crossed by laundry strung from one side to the other like bunting at a festival.

Everybody seemed to shout and gesticulate whether buying or selling but my uncle assured me that it was all good-natured bartering.

Why do I know the place so well? As my uncle and aunt had no children of their own, they borrowed me and took me there during school holidays for several years running.

In those days it took almost three days of car travel. Termoli was the height of exoticism, promising adventure and excitement, and I was very happy to go along.

My aunt and I would have enjoyed the occasional walk down the cobbled lanes to the beach and the 'New Town' but it was not encouraged, and we had to consider the good name of the family at all times. As we wanted a happy holiday, we gave in gracefully and showed gratitude whenever we were taken to a little beach outside town where the family kept their fishing boats. This gave my uncle the opportunity to show off his German built car, driving like a maniac through the little lanes. He was keen to demonstrate to the neighbours that working abroad had brought his family wealth and standing. Admittedly, the wealth was relative and hardly anything out of the ordinary in England but in the South of Italy it was cause for envy and admiration. My uncle, they had to admit, had done very well indeed!

Every year, Zio Gino was expected to bring a big present for the family, an ostentatious improvement to their house, something to impress neighbours and guests. The first year I went with them, it was a washing machine with an in-built dryer; the year after it was a dishwasher. Often these present created mayhem because the

Termoli plumber wasn't familiar with the installation of machines no one had ever seen before in these parts of Europe.

Before my third visit, uncle had sent ahead a whole new suite of British made flushing toilets, one for each floor of the house. By the time we arrived they had been installed and were proudly displayed to whoever came to the door.

Halfway into our holiday, disaster struck: the new toilets, the pride and joy of the family, flooded the entire ground floor and produced an unbelievable stench. The plumber, a man called Antonio, was summoned who of course, could find nothing wrong with his handiwork.

'You'll have to dig up the *Piazza Duomo*, follow the sewer pipes and see where they are blocked,' he said with menace to make sure no one expected him to do it.

After much gesticulating and shouting, *Mamma*, my uncle's mother, put on her formal black dress. This indicated a serious event. She usually only wore it for religious festivals, baptisms, weddings or funerals. She stormed off to do battle with the Mayor and returned triumphant from the *Municipio* waving a written permission to investigate the blockage. My uncle, his brothers and every able-bodied male relative were called to the scene and recruited to help with the excavation.

At the end of day one, a straight ditch with a pathetically thin sewer pipe lying at its bottom stretched from the house almost to the middle of the *Piazza*. *Mamma* was trying to placate the priest who had stormed across to them from his lavish residence to point out that there would be a *processione* on Sunday – in less than two days – from the church, across the square, through all the little lanes of old Termoli and back.

My aunt and I giggled at the thought that the whole *processione* might be so unobservant in their fervour that they might fall into the ditch. Nevertheless, *Mamma* promised that by then, the holes would be filled in.

Efforts were renewed the following morning, only to find that the entire sewage system ended in the middle of the *Piazza*. To the tut-tutting of the priest hanging out of one of his enormous windows and lots of head-shaking from neighbours tiptoeing across the building site, the pipe was quickly redirected at a sharp angle across the square and extended towards the edge of the cliff, so that the sewage could run down the rocky slope straight into the sparkling sea below.

While my uncle felt honour bound to help with digging, shovelling and plumbing, my aunt and I were left on the deserted beach by the families fishing boats. *Mamma* had prepared a picnic for our lunch but preferred to stay at home to supervise the men.

◻ ◻ ◻ ◻ ◻

'He didn't mean to become an immigrant worker,' Aunt Phyllis began the tale of their courtship, I had asked for so many times.

'He had no intention of staying in Europe. He and his friend Emilio had planned to emigrate to Australia. Somebody from the town gave them a lift to Rimini, and then they made their way across the Alps by train and hitch-hiking across Europe.

The plan was that they would first go to London where Emilio had a brother. The family had insisted that he say good-bye to him as well and that he should deliver presents from them; then the two young men from Termoli would take the ferry back to Hamburg where they would join a ship bound for Australia.'

On the second evening of their stay in England, Francisco, Emilio's brother, took them to a gathering of young church-goers.

'It was one of the few evenings,' my aunt recalled, 'that I was allowed out with my two elder sisters and my brother who was supposed to be our chaperon. I had expected the usual crowd from bible studies and Sunday school and not much fun. When we approached the church hall, we could hear modern music, and when we entered we saw a band playing and people dancing. My brother sat us down at one of the tables surrounding the dance floor, brought us a glass of lemonade each and disappeared. Later on we found out that that evening, he consolidated his acquaintance with his future wife.'

Aunt Phyllis smiled at the memory.

'We girls sat there watching everybody else and occasionally, when the band stopped we whispered to each other what we had observed. Suddenly, I caught a glimpse of two young foreign looking boys. They stood out with their healthy tan, dark, wavy hair, dancing eyes and wide grins. I couldn't get enough looking at them.' She almost swooned.

'I nearly died,' Auntie continued with a happy sigh, 'when one of them asked me for a dance. I remember it as if it was yesterday. How thrilled and awkward I felt at the same time!' And then she laughed out loud:

'It wore off quickly, though; definitely after the third and fourth dance. Well, my brother was nowhere to be seen, so I took full advantage.'

Auntie now began to unpack our picnic onto a table cloth which she had spread out over the sand. I was riveted and urged her to carry on with her story. She paused, sitting on her heels: 'At the end of the evening, Gino asked me for a date: You give to me, he said pointing at my beaded bracelet, I sure see you again!' she mimicked his heavy accent. 'I knew he was serious because his mouth was smiling but his eyes looked deeply into mine. I gave him the bracelet. Deep down, I was terribly worried what my stepmother would have to say about this.'

I was getting hungry and looked longingly at the picnic. However, my aunt was in full flow and carried on: 'Of course, my stepmother threw the expected tantrum, but when Gino came to the door, he overwhelmed her with his charm offensive and promised to bring me back safe and sound like an English gentleman would. He came every day, and for a while it felt as if he was wooing her. It had the desired effect: He became a constant in our lives and I was allowed to go out with him whenever I wanted. In return he helped her with repairs and decorating jobs in the house, or simply lifting heavy loads or shopping. All the while, he kept wearing my bracelet.'

'What happened to his friend Emilio?' I asked lying back on the sandy beach clasping my hands behind my head trying to stop my stomach from rumbling.

'He disappeared after a few days, fed up with waiting, and continued his way to Australia on his own.'

My aunt and I smiled at each other, she savouring the sweet memories, while I wallowed in the romantic notion of a teenager that this was the type of love every girl could expect when the right man came along.

'Gino soon found himself a job locally, and we met up most days after work. By that stage, I was a nursery assistant, and he had found work as a labourer on a building site.'

The sun stood at its zenith, bright and blistering making the sand sparkle like diamanté. While putting on our straw hats and sunglasses, she must have caught one of my longing glimpses at the tablecloth: 'You are hungry, of course! I am so sorry prattling on like this!'.

I assured my aunt that I was riveted but tucked in immediately. While munching on *ciabatta* rolls filled with Parma ham, followed by plump, juicy peaches, I urged her to continue with her tale and she willingly obliged:

'It was a time when guest workers from Italy were few and far between and not always welcome. They were expected to start at the lowest rung of any career ladder whatever their qualifications. Gino learnt English, a mixture of building site slang and his Southern Italian dialect. If he spoke fast, it sounded like a machine gun, and even I had sometimes trouble to keep up with him, but we were happy, and as long as we were just dating, my stepmother didn't mind. The problems only began, when Gino wanted to get engaged.'

At that point, we were interrupted. My uncle stomped across the beach towards the two of us, waving his arms and shouting from afar.

'You have to come home!'

He looked dirty, sweaty and a bit frightened what his wife would have to say about him deserting us for hours. For a few moments, she was playing at being cross, not with him but the family who hadn't got the toilets plumbed in properly in the first place and now expected him to repair them during his holiday. He listened for a bit with a bowed head like a naughty school boy; suddenly, he gave her a big hug, swirled her round the beach and finally kissed her hands and neck, laughing with relief when she finally laughed with him.

'We shall finish the work tomorrow,' he promised in the thick accent he had never shaken off.

And they did.

¤　¤　¤　¤　¤

Only a few days later, another drama ensued. It was my fault, the run-in with my uncle.

It was silly but as we were both stubborn it turned into a battle of wills.

We had gone into the New Town for uncle to change pounds into the then still existing *lire*. While waiting for him, I was chatted up by a nice boy with a French accent, about my age.

'You speak Engleeesh?' his voice was smooth as velvet. 'I am 'ere to visit famileee, but we live in Marseille.'

Neither I nor my aunt could see any harm in accepting an invitation for an ice cream at four o'clock in the afternoooon. He would wait for me outside the town wall.

We hadn't counted on my uncle's very different ideas when we pointed to the back of the nice young man walking away.

'You can't go out with him!' my uncle snapped.

'Why not?' I flicked my hair back in defiance. I didn't really care one way or another but being a teenager, this became a matter of principle.

'You belong to a *buona famiglia*' as if that alone settled the matter. 'You will not go!'

'We can all walk behind them, as we do on Sundays with Teresina…' my aunt mediated.

Teresina was my uncle's sister who was engaged to the best catch in town, a motor mechanic. Being engaged to be married, she had the great privilege of cooking for her beloved every afternoon under *Mamma's* supervision, and on Sundays, the young couple had permission to walk along the *frontemare*, the promenade, with the entire family following a few steps behind. Even holding hands was forbidden as it would have spoiled the girl's reputation.

How embarrassing, was my feeling but my aunt assured me that Teresina was happy to just show off her fiancé to the other girls.

Now I was in a similar predicament.

'At least I have to let him know,' I snapped.

'I take you there!' We drove the short distance to the town wall at five to four.

'What has he done that I can't meet him?' I aimed to sound recalcitrant.

'No more! Go and tell him!'

'You tell him then!' I could be as livid as he was.

'Good, I will!'

He stopped the car abruptly and rushed towards the young man who leant against the wall, smoking nervously. I watched my uncle as he gesticulated wildly and shouted something I couldn't hear. Then he stormed back to the car, threw himself into his seat, revved the engine angrily and drove off as if at the start of a Formula One race.

'What did you say to him?' I demanded to know, hanging on to the door handle for dear life. I suspected that he had been rude because I had seen my date fixing his eyes to the ground and grinding his cigarette stub into the pavement.

'If you must know,' my uncle scoffed, 'I told him: You know where you come from; you should know better! That's what I told him!'

'So where does he come from that it is such a crime?' I shouted at him as we reached the family home. My aunt came rushing out.

'The New Town!' my uncle shouted back and disappeared through the door. My aunt gave me a hug and put a finger to her lips indicating that I should leave it at that.

¤   ¤   ¤   ¤   ¤

The house was eerily quiet, so aunt Phyllis and I took refuge on the roof garden under the pergola overhung by vines and rapidly colouring red grapes. We heard somebody slam the door downstairs and saw Zio Gino rush across the Piazza.

'He'll do what all Italian men do when they feel guilty: Go to the *trattoria*, have an espresso or a beer and discuss politics with old friends,' she laughed.

'Where is everybody?' I asked.

'*Mamma* has gone to her room for a nap; *Bappo* is potterimg in his workshop and the rest of the family are either at work or gallivanting – looking for conquests amongst the tourists.'

We sat at the rickety round metal table, auntie with a glass of wine and me with home-made sugary lemonade with lots of lemon bits in it. I had calmed down. I did really love the drama of it all!

'You know,' my aunt resumed the story of their courtship, 'as soon as Gino proposed, my stepmother took a different stance. Suddenly Gino the welcome guest and adopted son was relegated to the role of foreigner, not quite good enough to become a fully-fledged member of the family.' She sighed with resignation.

It took months of negotiations, Auntie told me, and promises that they would stay in England, that he would never take his young wife to Italy to settle, and that they both would look after her in old age. As a carrot she dangled their inheritance: her detached three storey house with a big garden in an area where people were happy to just have a balcony.

To the young couple the house was not important, to be able to get married and live together, was.

'Promising to look after her in old age wasn't a big deal,' auntie said. 'I would have done that anyway. After all, she had brought us up after father's death.'

'We had a small wedding with only my stepmother, her priest, my sisters and my brother, my friend Elsie and Gino's favourite colleague John as best man. It was all a bit hush-hush, but we didn't care.'

Gino continued to work as a labourer, slogging his way up to *cappo*, group leader, while auntie trained further as a nursery nurse. In time she took over a local kindergarten. Their spare time consisted mainly in entertaining and amusing the stepmother in whose house they had been given the attic rooms. They felt obliged to take over most chores in the house and garden.

We sipped on our glasses. The oppressive heat of the day had vanished and been replaced by a more bearable warm sea breeze which enveloped us like a silk shawl.

'Can I try the grapes?'

'I wouldn't chance it. Look, they are still red. They need to be almost black before they can be picked.'

A shadow crossed her face. 'Our only regret was that we never had children. I would have so loved to have a little boy or girl with his looks…' I felt honoured that she discussed such a sensitive topic with me, treating me as an equal.

'Why didn't you?' I held my breath expecting her to give me a stern look. Instead she replied:

'I consulted all sorts of doctors, but it took me years to get Gino to have a test. It turned out that he had had the mumps as a teenager and was infertile. Of course, the family didn't believe the doctors and declared that it was still my fault. According to them, English women preferred to buy mod-cons, a big house and a big car to having children.'

At least nobody mentioned the matter again, and it remained a family secret.'

'It was all a long time ago…' she ended wistfully, stretching her arms above her head and supressing a yawn unsuccessfully.

'Time for bed!' she announced and gathered our glasses.

The last week of our holiday was highlighted by two things:

After my failed attempt at a date, I was given a chaperone, Zio's youngest brother Giovanni. My aunt was grateful that I would be away from our shared bedroom for a few hours each evening during which she hoped to salvage some privacy and holiday spirit with her husband.

I was happy to oblige until Giovanni displayed signs of completely misunderstanding his mission, introducing me to his mates as his *fidanzate**, who thereafter gave me respectful looks. It also unsettled me that he kept eyeing up engagement rings

* fiancée

104

in the window of the town's only jeweller. After I had to fend off more and more passionate advances, I decided to stay closer to home, however disappointed my aunt would be. They must have guessed because Giovanni disappeared for the rest of our stay.

On my last night of the holiday, I stayed up on the roof top until the stars came out, the birds had stopped singing and the town below prepared for sleep. Finally returning to the bedroom, hearing the regular breathing of my uncle and aunt, and crawling almost noiselessly in total darkness to my bed, I lost one of my contact lenses, only to find it trodden on in the morning. By now I was glad to leave even though I had to endure the return journey via Rome, which I had so looked forward to, one-eyed and with blurred vision.

◻ ◻ ◻ ◻ ◻

'*Cara mia!*' Zio Gino now shouts from the kitchen. 'I shall make-a the best Bolognese you have ever eaten!' His enthusiasm and exuberance have never dimmed.

'Aha, time for a girlie chat!' My aunt leans across the table: 'Any news?' she whispers like a conspirator.

'You never told me the end of your story.' I evade her question.

'Well, there isn't much left to tell. My stepmother grew old. She really exploited us but I didn't see it like that, and Gino was far too good-hearted to complain. For a long time, we felt as if we were on borrowed time, that sooner or later someone would withdraw that permission. He had to work harder than his English colleagues, be a better husband, a better son-in-law than any Englishmen would have been. I often felt sorry for him, but he didn't want to talk about it. It would have hurt his pride. He used to say: As long as I am with you, I don't mind anything.'

Since my stepmother died, we have a bit more freedom and a bit more money. We sold the house and bought this flat. But we have grown older, too, and now his health is deteriorating…'

'What happened to his family?'

'We haven't been there for years, but we ring occasionally. Both his parents are dead and his brothers and Teresina have already grandchildren themselves. They all live in the New Town. Recently they had an earthquake and ended up sheltering in the garage, the only place they trust because they have built it themselves. But otherwise, life hasn't changed much: Still births, marriages and deaths,' she laughs.

I chew nervously on my lower lip; I need some reassurance: 'Auntie, do you think it was all worthwhile?' She raises her eyebrows as if she doesn't understand my question. When I remain silent, she answers:

'Of course, it was! What a silly question!' She looks at me with a suspicious grin as if something dawns on her, 'Why do you ask?'

'Well, I met this man from Greece…'

She leans back and bursts out laughing:

'You dark horse! Now, you must tell me all about him!'

'*Mangiare…la cena!*' come the excited shouts from the kitchen: dinner is ready.

As we walk through to the dining room, she squeezes my shoulders in solidarity.

'Your niece is in love,' she announces. Zio Gino puts the bowl heaped with pasta down on the table and throws his arms around me.

'*Bravissimo, mia cara!* At last!'

RIVALS

RIVALS

Oh God! I wish I didn't have to ring her. I can't stand her which is not surprising: She ruined my life and that of my children! She has stolen what was most precious to us, but the odd thing is that she has always managed to make me feel the guilty party.

He was **my** husband!

Now that he is dead I must stop her from stealing the rest.

Where is my address book? What a long number to dial from London to Dhaka. My hands are shaking.

'Sultana?'

¤   ¤   ¤   ¤   ¤

Hold on, I first have to dry my hands.

'Sultana speaking.'

Oh no! Not Jennifer! What does she want from me? At a time like this! How cruel! She is the last person I want to talk to right now.

¤   ¤   ¤   ¤   ¤

My voice has gone. I must try to focus on what I have to say – but all the memories come flooding back:

When I met Rashid I was working in banking and had made it

to manageress in no time. I was efficient, meticulous, good with people and – let's face it, it is important – well-groomed, even attractive. Meeting him at the height of my career and learning to divide my attention between ambition and our relationship was, to say the least, tricky. Nevertheless, we got married. I worked through pregnancy and even maternity leave just to keep my job; after all I was supporting my unemployed husband. He went to evening language classes to improve his chances of a job. Once our little girl was born, I asked for part-time work. As expected it was refused and pointed out that it would scupper any further career prospects. So I returned to work full time.

Meanwhile, my husband planned a journey home funded by my earnings, not even considering whether Leila, our daughter, and I wanted to come along.

'It's not good for her health; she is so little,' I remember him drawing himself up to his full height. When that didn't impress me, he lowered the tone of his voice and explained gently like to a stubborn child:

'It's far too hot. You are not used to that sort of temperature.' I was torn between the belief that he cared and the suspicion that he much rather went on his own.

And finally he argued: 'We haven't got enough money for all three of us to go.'

Considering that I was the breadwinner, I should have gone and left him behind.

'I spend all year in your country; I miss my brothers and sisters, and my father is old and not very well…' which was true but no consolation. In the end, I gave in.

My husband began to make enquiries how to have a fridge shipped to Bangladesh,

'A fridge is as expensive as my flight ticket!' I protested.

He looked puzzled as if he didn't quite understand my point.

When it finally dawned on him, he accused me of being mean, as this was a one-off gesture of thanks to the family; what for he didn't say.

I obviously couldn't win, so I decided to be kind and understanding, to give him the benefit of the doubt. It didn't come easy!

The fridge was sent off. Soon afterwards, my husband followed.

¤   ¤   ¤   ¤   ¤

I wonder why she pauses but it gives me time to gather my thoughts.

The line is crackling... oh good, it has broken down.

How often have I wished that he had never set eyes on Jennifer! We were perfectly happy the way we were but she spoilt it all.

The village I grew up in was tiny and the school an hour's walk away. People slogged their hearts out to grow rice and vegetables, weaving baskets or embroidering saris. Everyone was poor; everyone struggled to make a living and to feed the many mouths. Education was secondary and a luxury, particularly for girls. They were trained to be housewives; once they had reached puberty, they would be married off. I was married at fourteen to a man double my age... Bulbul seemed to be kind, had a good job and soon took me to live in the capital, but he wasn't very interested in me as a person.

Bulbul came from a good family; some were in business and others in the Civil Service. Sometimes he was scathing about something he called 'nepotism'. When he explained, I couldn't see anything wrong with wanting to better oneself. In a poor country like ours you have to grab your chances.

Soon after we were married, my husband announced that his two younger brothers would move in with us. Of course, I felt sorry that the boys' mother had died prematurely, but at fifteen, I did not feel ready to take her place: Karim was a stroppy twelve year old, while his brother Rashid was two years older and a quiet, serious boy. For the first couple of weeks, they kept to themselves in the room they shared. The servants reported that they had drawn a chalk line through the middle of the windowless room to indicate where each private space began and ended. I never entered it; it wouldn't have been proper.

The airless flat with its corridors like rabbit warrens had rubbed off the shine of city life for me and sometimes I thought with nostalgia of the light-flooded huts in my village surrounded by lush green paddy fields and wooded hills, but I counted my blessings.

My husband was rarely at home; he was a high ranking police officer, first posted in the city, then after a promotion, all around the country. I was left with my two charges. They went to school and I encouraged them to study hard. Karim continued to keep his distance, but Rashid became an easy companion who made me laugh and let me participate in his studies. I learnt more supervising his homework than I had ever learnt in the village school.

Soon I suspected that I was pregnant. The boys were farmed out to another auntie while I was giving birth at home; my husband came for a quick look, and the boys were returned to our household.

Rashid became my support, my backbone, my defender. Lying there with my little girl nuzzling into the crook of my elbow, I realised that I had missed him more than I had ever missed my husband. I had fallen in love. Of course, I couldn't confide in anybody; I didn't even dare to admit it to myself. So I concentrated on being motherly to all three of them. I was still only sixteen.

My husband had increased our domestic staff including a cook, two servants and an ayah who took some of the burdens off my shoulders. I loved sitting with Rashid talking about his studies; he was the open door to a world of learning. It was sweet of him to say that I was at least as intelligent as he was.

During his time at College, I became aware that rumours circulated in the family but I took no notice. We were not doing anything wrong.

Soon Rashid had his first marriage proposal – maybe the family tried to get him away from me. The photograph he showed me was that of a well-made-up beauty, smiling coquettishly at the camera. He was told that she came from a wealthy and well-reputed family of doctors in Dhaka. My heart sank. Rashid laughed at me and assured me that he wasn't ready for marriage.

Still, I had to go to bed for a few days with a thumping headache and stomach cramps until he promised that he would reject the offer.

We both realised that we had become inseparable, necessary to each other like the air we breathed. I had no hesitation in 'becoming his very own in an act of deepest affection' as he put it. We spent the following weeks in a happy delirium and I couldn't have cared less what the world was about to say.

Word must have reached my husband in a far-away corner of the country. He suddenly turned up, furious, suspicious and domineering. He issued orders all day long and scowled like a bad tempered sniffer dog. He polluted the already sticky air in the flat with his chain-smoking which made me gag and cough, and fear that the baby might get a chest infection.

My headaches and stomach pains returned and I had to have frequent lie-downs.

My husband left as suddenly as he had arrived.

The gossip blossomed but I had become immune to criticism, and Rashid defended my honour hotly whenever people talked about me in a derogatory manner. We became secretive and circumspect.

My husband rarely returned and took to sending me the housekeeping money via a banking order. He took little interest in our first born and even less in our second. Well, even I wasn't sure whether it was his; officially it was.

My heart broke, when the family put pressure on Rashid to finish his studies abroad. Karim, his brother, had by that time become completely unmanageable and was removed from my care to live with another auntie. For a few blissful weeks, Rashid and I had the flat to ourselves, lived like husband and wife, but we both knew that the dream would soon end.

¤   ¤   ¤   ¤   ¤

I don't believe it: The telephone lines still have a habit of breaking up. In a way, it's a blessing. I am paralysed. Sultana's voice still gives me the creeps.

I better wait a few minutes until I have my feelings under control. This is not personal, it's business. I must think of my children!

For as long as Rashid and I lived in England it was taken for granted that I was going to work to earn as much money as possible. As soon as I returned home in the evenings, I metamorphosed into a Bengali housewife, put on my cotton *sari* and cooked my husband's favourite meals.

A further trip home was planned. Again Rashid insisted on a big shipment, another fridge. He owned up that it was for a particular member of the family, his brother's wife, who was struggling financially. My sarcastic question, how many fridges she needed, fell on deaf ears. I didn't really mind because this time I would go with him. I didn't want to spoil the anticipation with jealousy. Even I got carried away buying presents for about forty nieces and nephews, filling a suitcase until it bulged.

About mid-summer I realised that I had fallen pregnant again, and I was discouraged from travelling, not so much by my doctor but by my husband. He worried that the short span between the pregnancies, the long journey, the different climate, food and surroundings might harm my health. As I had never been to Bangladesh I had no idea whether his concerns were justified.

He promised to be back in time for the birth. In the event, he just missed it. At least it was the longed-for son.

I must dial again.

◘   ◘   ◘   ◘   ◘

Will she ring again? I hope not!

She was not one of us; he found her abroad, and he married her.

Suddenly, the family was abuzz with wedding news; some even travelled to England to inspect and welcome her into the family. I heard of a lavish white wedding in a castle paid for by Jennifer's wealthy parents.

My life came to a shuddering halt. I kept myself to myself and suffered in silence. By then I had developed stomach ulcers amongst other complaints. My husband had accepted a post in a far flung corner of the country and didn't want me to follow him.

Rashid and his new wife had two children in quick succession, one unfortunately a son and heir. I didn't really want to know all the details. I had never been to England and could not imagine him in a foreign country living with foreign people, cut off from his roots. I guess he stayed there to please her. The first time he came back to visit was without her. He sent the gift of a fridge to my house, as if that would compensate for the hurt he had caused me. I didn't need alms!

Rashid must have heard that I was ailing, because the next time he came for a home visit he sent another fridge for me and came to inspect it. He had thought that I might be able to sell it to have some extra money. So sweet!

However, he couldn't be quite as loving as he had been in the past. Her ghost stood between us!

'Sultana,' he said when he finally brought her to my house on

the third visit, 'this is Jennifer.' I was glad, that he didn't add 'my wife', I would have died on the spot.

Jennifer was pretty in an insipid sort of way; skinny; pale complexion; watery blue eyes; short, blond hair; if she had been any taller she would have towered over him.

She made an effort to fit in – she wore saris and ate all the food without complaint and pretended to be kind and caring, but there was something steely in her eyes. I didn't take to her and thought it scandalous the way she joked and flirted with the men in the family. She laughed a lot and with every peal she flicked her hair like a teenager trying to impress the boys.

I dreaded her visits to my house. She would enquire about my health and show false compassion. I didn't want her there, particularly not with him! I didn't need her kindness!!

I could see in Rashid's eyes that he hoped we two women would become friends. How could he! She had stolen him from me!

¤   ¤   ¤   ¤   ¤

I need some more time before I can ring again… I am still shaking.

I finally made it to Bangladesh proudly presenting our two children to the family. I was received with such warmth and generosity, almost drowning in the sweet smelling flower garlands round my neck that I began to wonder what all the fuss had been about. Chauffeurs were delegated to drive me – with a chaperone, of course – wherever I wanted to go. I was fed on heavenly curries, spicy but not hot, syrupy sweetmeats and exotic ice creams made with mango and pistachio. No wonder, I put on a few pounds which I could hide easily under the colourful, floating saris.

I was helped to dress every morning. My nieces wanted to show off their Western auntie. To their horror, I tanned quite easily and soon looked not much different to them. Only my blond bob set me apart which developed almost white streaks and began to look like a wig.

Our children loved having so many cousins to play with or being carried around by an *ayah*. I could relax knowing that everyone was safe and entertained.

I didn't see much of my husband and imagined that he would meet up with brothers and friends. It was probably customary. I ignored gentle digging by one of his sisters about his frequent absences and her impish speculation whether 'he was inspecting the fridges'.

I had observed that Muslim society was close knit; there wouldn't be any room for mischief; the whole city would soon know about it. I scolded myself for even entertaining such unkind thoughts.

It was hard to discover that my trust had been misplaced!

¤　　¤　　¤　　¤　　¤

I was astonished when after their return to England he began to correspond again, little reports of his life in a strange world, snippets about his substitute family. He sounded homesick. I kept the letters in bundles and tied them lovingly with pink ribbons.

After several years, they finally moved to Bangladesh. I wasn't sure whether to be elated or afraid. What would be expected of me? To watch the happy couple from afar or to be his first love again?

Eventually it turned out to be the latter.

Of course, their marriage didn't last. I heard through the grapevine that Rashid and his English wife fought like cat and dog. He never gave anything away, and it would have been foolish of me to press him.

Suddenly, the shocking news reached me that Jennifer had left the country with the children and had filed for divorce.

Rashid was devastated. Under Islamic law, the children stay with the father, but the British court only gave him limited visiting rights. He was also supposed to pay maintenance, but it was unenforceable over that distance.

It took a year until he came to terms with the situation, cut his losses and returned to my arms for good.

¤   ¤   ¤   ¤   ¤

I still can't get myself to ring again. Shall I drop the whole idea of staking our claim?

At first I thought, everybody was totally wrong about Sultana. She wouldn't be Rashid's type: swarthy, scarred from bad acne; her unusually thin black hair stretched back into a meagre bun; her heavy-lidded eyes overhung by thick eyebrows like a threatening avalanche; a narrow forehead, the wide nose and thin lips like lines drawn with a ruler, rarely smiling, never laughing. She was a sullen woman, and my husband wouldn't be interested in her!

There was one thing, however, which had stuck in my mind. 'I owe her,' my husband had said. She certainly knew how to arouse pity. It was sickening how Rashid fussed around her; he had never fussed over me. Neither I nor the doctor ever found out what exactly was wrong with her.

It couldn't be that bad as she had bothered to plaster her bad skin in foundation, coloured her almost none-existent mouth with bright red lipstick and made her mascara-ed lashes look like stuck together spider legs. By the time we arrived at her house she had retired to her bed sighing and moaning.

I did make an effort to be pleasant, fawning over her like my husband did, but there was an impenetrable glacier between us which my compassion could not melt. The two of them were so obviously wincing at my presence that, in the end, I decided not to visit her again.

The more I watched Rashid and Sultana, the more I got confused. Where was her husband? I met him on family gatherings and he seemed nice, funny and charming. Moreover, he had a good job in the Police Service, which is a piece of good fortune in such a poor country. However, I never saw his wife with him.

'You have not yet explained to me why you owe her,' I began my calm offensive on the one rare occasion when Rashid and I were alone.

He launched immediately into a tirade of aggressive defence: 'My relatives have put you up to this! They are jealous and have turned you against me!'

I was taken aback: 'That's not true. I am simply trying to understand why Sultana has this elevated status, why you give her preferential treatment.'

He was beside himself: 'You will never be like her! She is an angel, but you wouldn't understand that!' after which he stormed out of the house, presumably to find solace with her.

I obviously could not win.

Self-preservation told me not to wait until my self-doubts had undermined my confidence to an extent where I would just give in. After a period of despair and soul-searching, I filed for divorce while visiting my parents in England. I had been well aware that, had I announced such a drastic step in Bangladesh, I would have lost the children to their father.

It took some acting to ask for permission to travel under the pretext of giving us all a bit of breathing space. In truth, I felt numb and immensely sad, leaving the family behind without saying good-bye, never mind facing up to my shattered dreams and a life as a divorcee and single mother.

As Sultana was obviously the love of his life, he could now spend as much time with her as he wanted.

What was her telephone number again?

¤   ¤   ¤   ¤   ¤

Oh no, she is ringing again. Shall I pick up the receiver? I can't face her right now. I shall let it ring for a bit...

During the time of our reunion, I could hear the collective sigh of distress of his relatives. I didn't care. My heart was singing. No one had sided with me while he was married; no one had cared how I was feeling. Now I would turn the tables: I would subtly keep him away from them.

Rashid was more upset by the divorce than he let on, I could see it in his frowns, but we never discussed it.

He bought a large flat for us in a beautiful district of Dhaka where we lived for the next twenty-five years – outcasts, yes, but happy in our own little world. If he ever visited his sisters or brothers, he never mentioned them, and I didn't enquire. I was determined that none of them would ever cross the threshold of our home.

My health improved and my suffering was at an end.

Two of our children lived with us until they got married, and then he bought flats for them as well. The others moved abroad; and my husband Bulbul died about fifteen years ago.

Every couple of years, we had a hectic visit from Rashid's sons who were well-mannered in a British sort of way. They were malleable, easy to flatter and no trouble.

Now that Rashid has died, I have every reason to fear them; or more to the point, to fear their mother.

¤   ¤   ¤   ¤   ¤

'Sultana, let's talk before the line breaks up again. The children want to come over for the funeral.'

'There is no need. The burial is tomorrow.'

'Please, have it postponed. He was their father!'

120

'I see what I can do.' I have no intention of even trying.

'Please, do your best. They would be heart-broken'.

They have been very good in keeping in contact with him, and have even chosen professions he wanted for them, doctor and lawyer. The power of emotional blackmail!

'How do you know that Rashid died?'

'His brother Karim rang me.'

I thought as much! 'What did he tell you?'

'That Rashid had a stroke.'

I wonder whether he mentioned anything else...

'Did he leave a will, Sultana?' *I am sure he did; he was always a stickler for order.*

'No', even I can hear what a lame answer that is. 'He didn't expect to die so soon, Jennifer.'

She is lying! 'Well, it doesn't matter right now.'

'What do you mean?' Fear strikes my heart.

'I am sure you know that even if there is no will, his legitimate children are his heirs.'

Damn Karim! She wouldn't have known that her children are entitled to my flat, our children's flats, his sizeable bank account. Oh my God! 'There isn't a lot to inherit...' *I mumble feebly.*

'That remains to be established officially, Sultana, but we are not heartless; we won't drive you out of your home! We understand that this is hard for you, too.'

Although you deserve it – is what I really want to say. I almost lose control of my emotions but I force myself to remain calm, logical and business-like.

This is giving me a splitting headache Not drive me out of my home? She can't – or can she? I am sure I have more right to be his widow. and I am beginning to feel sick. I must lie down!

'I don't want your understanding,' I sob. 'I lost my husband.'

'So did I, Sultana, so did I!'

KAZUO

KAZUO

Kazuo stops reading the newspaper and walks over to the floor-to-ceiling window of his 20th storey apartment in the Shinjuky area of Tokyo. He stares out without seeing the familiar view of futuristic towers around him which he, as an architect, often admires. In fact, normally his heart swells with pride because he was involved in the construction of some of them.

However, today he looks blankly towards the sky, his thoughts lost in the past.

¤　¤　¤　¤　¤

Kazuo had grown up in a traditional Japanese family. His father was the technical director of a big car manufacturer. His mother was a housewife organising her life around that of her husband and her son, keeping their beautiful house on the hill spotless and cooking meals to welcome the two of them back every evening.

The boy never questioned whether his parents were happy. There was never one word louder than the other; if discussions were necessary – if ever they happened, for all he knew – they were hushed and conducted far from his ears.

Kazuo was a single child, precious, precocious and groomed to fulfil the expectations of his parents. And he didn't disappoint.

He loved the house he grew up in, the beauty of it, the structure; the well-thought-out features which made life comfortable. They even had a tiny Zen garden – almost a miracle amongst the buildings jostling for every square inch. His mother tended it lovingly.

To the delight of his parents, Kazuo mapped out his future early on: He wanted to become someone who created buildings, homes with a warm atmosphere, maybe a little warmer than the one he had grown up in.

When he tried to explain this to his mother once, getting a little carried away at the prospect, he noticed a shadow crossing her face as if he had criticised her.

He never touched on a personal subject again, but decided with the passion and impulsiveness of youth that he had to take every opportunity coming his way. He wanted to be the best, for himself and for them.

Kazuo jumped at the chance when he was awarded a grant to study architecture for a whole year in England. Naturally, he was thrilled, excited beyond measure like any young person would have been. His parents were proud and happy for him, but also slightly apprehensive. What would the influences be? Would they change their beloved, dutiful son? Would he come back? This last thought was too unbearable to consider.

He promised them, that he would keep in constant contact; that he would share with them all his experiences and, of course, he would return.

¤   ¤   ¤   ¤   ¤

It was the first flight Kazuo had ever undertaken, and such a long one at that. To him it was a great adventure. He looked forward to progressing in his studies, learning about methods of architects before him, to be encouraged to develop his own ideas and to test them under the scrutiny of experienced teachers. It was also a wonderful opportunity to partake in a different culture, to see how other people lived and what sort of homes they built for themselves; if he was very lucky, he would be able to do some networking and to make friends.

He settled into his student life in London with ease: He was totally engrossed in his lessons and attended each and every one listed on his timetable. In his spare time, he went to London's wonderful museums and couldn't believe that most didn't charge for the entrance. He shared a house with two other male students who were a little messy and seemed to attend more parties than lectures, but it was none of his business and in a way advantageous because he had the house to himself and could study without disturbance.

And then, one day, life changed beyond all recognition. He met Mimi.

They had both attended what had been advertised as 'a function' organised by the most prestigious art college in town, which however, turned out to be an informal affair for which they were both overdressed. She stood in a corner in a dark blue satin dress with a white lace collar looking out of the window as if she were very lonely and longing to be outside. Kazuo in his dark suit and bow tie had observed her for a while when one of the college lecturers spoke to her; the man had to stoop to hear her.

From then onwards she had stood almost motionless by the window, ignoring the noisy, exuberant crowd.

He knew exactly how she felt standing there at the other end of the room, out of place, superfluous, isolated. He made his way slowly across to her, gently nudging people to let him pass through.

When he finally stood before her, shyness befell him and he could only smile.

She smiled back.

It was the beginning of a gentle, disciplined friendship without emotional outbursts; any problems were sensibly discussed and fairly solved. He sometimes suspected that being so placid Mimi surely must have some Japanese ancestry in her background. All he really knew was that she had British parents who lived in France.

She was to him both familiar and exciting.

After several dates of movies, dinners and walks in the countryside Mimi suggested tentatively that he move in with her. She lived in a tiny terraced house which her parents had bought for her.

He was taken aback that she was willing to cohabit without being married to him, without any pressure to commitment, not even demanding a token ring.

Everything was so much easier, freer in the West; young people were not encumbered by conventions and the traditional values of their elders.

He avoided thinking about his parents back in Tokyo and certainly didn't inform them about his new address and the enormous step he had taken in his personal development.

Kazuo and Mimi ticked along nicely, cheerfully working towards their final examinations, he in architecture, and she in art history. He even learnt to enjoy household chores; he felt thoroughly westernised.

He never thought about what would happen when his student visa ran out; he suspected that the practical solution would be to get married. This however, had to wait until he could afford to provide for a family.

A thunderbolt struck his pleasant existence when Mimi announced that she was pregnant. He was in total shock! This news obliterated his peaceful life, his easy trust, and burnt everything to a cinder.

Why hadn't she taken precautions? How could he ever return home now? In such disgrace! How would he tell his parents who expected him to become the most famous architect in Japan; who would at the height of his success marry a Japanese lady with superior credentials? He panicked like a trapped animal. Was there an alternative?

When he looked at Mimi's face he realised that her radiant smile had turned into a bitterly disappointed frown. They were so well attuned; she had read his thoughts.

'Get out.' She whispered with steel in her words.

He went upstairs to pack his things.

He found a room for the last three months of his bursary and spent his lonely evenings mourning his loss. He tried to contact Mimi several times to patch things up, but his attempts were half-hearted and she put the phone down as soon as she heard his voice. Would it make things better if he proposed? But how could he if she didn't even listen to him?

He passed his examinations with distinction and returned to Japan before the end of term celebrations began. He felt like a thief sneaking out of the country.

¤　¤　¤　¤　¤

Kazuo returned to the fold of his family to the expected applause. Soon Tokyo society discovered his talent and after only a few years, Kazuo Ogawa became one of the most renowned creators of elegant high-rise buildings and family residences alike. He was involved in the planning and execution of Odaibo, a man-made island in the South of the city and the futuristic towers subsequently built on it.

He had brought honour to the family name. He never told his parents that there was a chance that they had become grand-parents.

As his career flourished and his fame spread, he was asked to travel all over the world, on business, to lead projects or to collect awards.

He tried several times to find Mimi, and – as he hoped – his child. He didn't even know whether it was a boy or girl or whether ultimately Mimi had decided to have an abortion.

Not surprisingly, she didn't live at her old address any more, and nobody seemed to know where she had gone. Someone thought that they had last seen her with a toddler; a little girl, they thought, but weren't sure.

As the years passed, his parents died, one shortly after the other, and he reached a point where the idea of marriage and children became less urgent, even uninteresting, like the peak of a surfing wave flattening out on the shore.

The knowledge of having fathered a child far away was buried deep in his soul; on the rare occasion that he thought about it, it hurt but he had learnt to suppress the image. Only very occasionally did he allow himself to muse what had become of his son or daughter. Did he or she know about him or had all traces of his relationship with their mother been expunged? Was his child perhaps totally immersed in European or American culture?

¤   ¤   ¤   ¤   ¤

It was yesterday's music programme on radio that had brought it all back: A young pianist from England spoke about a concert she was going to give in one of the most beautiful halls in Tokyo, the Suntory Hall. He knew and loved it; it had been the passion of its founder Keizo Saji, whose dream was to arrange the audience around the musicians, 'like vines facing the sun', and thus enveloping the listeners with the most perfect sound.

He applauded the young woman's choice of venue.

The programme she was going to perform tempted him: Debussy's *A l'Apres-Midi d'un Faune*, Chopin's *Preludes no.11* and finally the Beethoven *Emperor Concerto*. Pretty impressive for one evening, he thought.

He had again heard and seen her this morning on breakfast television. He was surprised. He remembered the gentle, accent-free English voice from the radio but on screen she didn't look English at all: She had Japanese eyes, silky, straight, black hair down to her waist and a porcelain complexion. She was in her late twenties he guessed, had studied at the Guildhall School of Music in London and was hailed the most promising young artist of the year.

130

He listened attentively to what she had to say about the concert and her meteoric rise to classical music stardom.

In the middle of the interview the programme's presenter changed the subject:

'I understand that you also have a personal reason to come to Tokyo?'

'I am looking for my father,' the pianist almost choked with emotion and then continued to appeal to anyone amongst the viewers and listeners to help her find him.

'All I know is that he is Japanese,' she said, 'in his fifties; he has at one time studied architecture in London and was known by the name of Kazuo.'

'Please, come forward', she pleaded, 'come to my concert tonight at the Suntory Hall. A complementary ticket will be waiting for you at the box office... And after the concert,' – at which point her eyes filled with tears – 'I hope you will come backstage so we can meet.

Kazuo turns slowly away from the view over his beloved Tokyo and looks at today's newspaper on the sofa which he has kept open at the page of the advertisement for the piano concert of Nishiko Jones. Nishiko means 'child of the West'. Mimi had chosen well.

Kazuo has been in two minds all day, but now he looks at the pianist's picture one last time, dials the box office number and confirms that he will attend.

Then he rings the florist and orders an armful of roses to be sent.

'Any message?' asks the florist as a matter of routine.

'Yes, please write: For my wonderful daughter, my 'child of the West', from her father Kazuo Ogawa.

USCHI

USCHI

The two women met in a children's playground.

One was petite, thin almost, her brown hair tucked behind her ears, an aquiline nose and heart-shaped mouth, She was dressed in tight blue-jeans and a pink T-shirt, a yummy mummy long before it was fashionable to call her that.

'Very pretty', thought Uschi who sat at the other end of the same bench. She hated her bulky, ungainly body, her big bosoms and thick waist. She felt frumpy and sweaty in her long-sleeved, flower-patterned blouse and the woollen grey skirt whose straining waistband was obscured by a long, grey cardigan.

Her bench companion seemed to be engrossed in a paperback, occasionally looking up in the direction of the sandpit.

'What lovely big, brown eyes.' Uschi thought. Hers were grey-green and bulging behind thick rimmed glasses.

'You read,' Uschi said to the yummy mummy the next time she looked up. 'I'll look out for them. Which one is yours?'

'Those two boys over there,' she said and added with gratitude: 'That is very nice of you!'

The two little boys looked nothing like their mother from a distance. They were of two different shades of brown. Their father was obviously a foreigner. They were lovely, one about two, the other only slightly older; they could even be twins. Both had thick black hair, cut in the style the Beatles used to wear in their heyday. From afar they appeared to be rumbustious little lads, chasing each other while shrieking with laughter. After a while, they seemed to settle with other children in the sandpit and made childish efforts to integrate in the existing castle-building and cake baking community.

'Lively, but no trouble,' Uschi thought, her gaze sweeping over to the sandpit corner where her daughter, four year old Amina, sat. The little girl was deeply concentrating on filling up her bucket with sand and emptying it again.

Both women were interrupted in their thoughts and reading when the boys rushed up to the bench, the little one struggling to keep up.

'They won't let us play!' they complained bitterly as only disappointed children can do. Their mother shut the book, put it next to her on the bench and gave them her attention:

'Did you ask nicely?' she enquired less concerned with the complaint than questioning their behaviour. Both nodded emphatically.

'We did ask nicely, but they said no'. They felt really hard done by.

'Maybe they were in the middle of a game?'

'No, they weren't.' The boys were convinced that the others had been out of order.

'You can play with each other, the two of you!'

'Would you like to play with my daughter,' interrupted the woman at the other end of the bench. 'See the little girl over there in the corner on her own? That's Amina. She'll play with you.'

Without even looking at their mother again, they rushed off in the direction indicated, shrieking anew with excitement.

The two women saw little Amina look up in surprise from her bucket at the whirlwind intruders, and then the boys settled each on either side of her and helped her with the task, one shovelling sand with a plastic trowel, the other holding the bucket and Amina having the privilege of emptying it all out again.

Amina looked a little like her new playmates, dark curls falling around her cute round face, large brown eyes and olive skin which, on a colour scale, fitted somewhere between that of the boys.

'Thank you; that was very kind,' said the yummy mummy gratefully.

'That's alright. Look how nicely they play together. They look like three peas in a pot...' Both women burst out laughing.

'I am Mia,' the yummy mummy introduced herself.

'I am Uschi.' They shook hands and moved closer together.

'I hope you don't mind me asking... where is your husband from?'

Mia grinned as if caught doing something naughty.

'Bangladesh,' she said hesitantly; nobody ever knew where that was.

'Gosh, and I thought, I had made an exotic choice. Mine is from Turkey.'

'No wonder they don't look like any of the others.' Mia nodded in the direction of the little gaggle of their children.

'Are you coming here often?'

'Yes, most days.'

'We only just moved here,' Mia explained. 'Will you be coming tomorrow?'

'Yes, I am pretty sure,' and they agreed that it would be nice to meet up again.

As it happened the weather turned on day three of their acquaintance and having exchanged telephone numbers Mia rang and invited Uschi and Amina to her flat instead.

'Are you sure?' Uschi seemed to worry about something.

'Of course I am. The children can play together, and we can sit in the warm and have a coffee.'

'Sounds heavenly,' Uschi agreed. 'I'll bring some cake; I have baked one this morning.'

'Great! I am afraid I usually nip to the baker's on the corner. I am no good at baking.'

The visit was a success and Mia only regretted that she had to ask her guests to leave at 5 o'clock in anticipation of her husband's return from work. He would expect the place to be neat and tidy and would insist on peace and quiet after a stressful day. Every day she rushed around with the hoover through their three large rooms – a sitting room which doubled up as a dining room, the master bedroom and the children's room –and the carpeted landing to make sure everything was perfect before he arrived. He was used to having servants in Bangladesh who would keep everything in tip-top condition and would produce the most delicious meals. In England they couldn't afford a cleaner or a cook so these tasks fell to his wife. It had been funny to watch his horrified face when he had enquired about hourly rates; in Bangladesh servants were grateful to be taken on at all and required nothing more than accommodation, meals and a laughable amount of money which they sent home to help their families in the villages.

Mia didn't mind being a housewife and mother. She had every intention to return to her career as a well-paid translator once the boys were old enough for school. Now she was at home all day, a clean house and a warm dinner on the table was the least her husband could expect.

She suspected that he found life in the West hard going.

'My husband is no different,' Uschi reassured her when ushered out with apologies while her daughter skipped already down the stairs.

'It was such a lovely afternoon! Next time you must come to us.'

Mia found Uschi's home quite different from her modern, airy place. It was in a Victorian town house split up into flats. The ceilings were high with cornices and plaster mouldings and a huge round rosette in the middle from which hung a white Japanese paper lantern. In Victorian times a much grander chandelier would presumably have been suspended. Everything was bathed in gloomy shadows.

These huge rooms must be murder to heat, thought Mia, feeling the draft swishing through the gaps underneath the doors.

Her boys, however, loved Amina's spacious playroom filled with stacks of toys which were a little girlie perhaps but her new friends were gracious and didn't mention it.

'My husband spoils her rotten,' said Uschi with a sigh. 'She is our only child and the apple of his eye.'

Seeing that the children were settled and absorbed in their play, the women retreated to the lounge to have a chat. There was a lot to talk about.

They were both local girls. Uschi's parents had already died many years ago, while Mia was still supervised by hers. They lived round the corner from her flat and saw it as their duty to interfere frequently in their daughter's marriage. They had been greatly concerned when she had introduced Rahim and had only given their blessings after he had promised that the young couple would settle close-by and that he would not ever move back to Bangladesh. Rahim had given them his word and they had subsequently paid for a lavish wedding inviting all their friends to gloss over the fact that they were a little embarrassed about their daughter's choice of husband. They needed to demonstrate that they were broadminded and cosmopolitan. In truth they were eager to suffocate any rumours that a rift had developed in the family.

'What they really thought was that I should have found a nice English boy; after all I had had plenty of offers,' Mia giggled asking for another piece of Uschi's delicious chocolate cake.

'I had none of that trouble,' Uschi took up the thread. 'Just as well my parents were dead before I met Kamal. They would never have approved! My father tended to sympathise with the Far Right. My marrying a Turk would have broken his heart.'

'Where did you meet your husband?' Mia asked wiping crumbs from her lips with a paper napkin.

'At a tea dance. I was dragged there by a well-meaning friend. I was convinced that nobody would take any notice of me.'

'Oh come on!' Mia was shocked at her friend's low opinion of herself. Uschi wasn't what one would term conventionally good-looking, but she had a lovely personality, a kind heart and a great sense of humour.

'Well, I certainly didn't expect anybody to dance with me but Kamal homed in on me and even asked me for a date afterwards.'

'For a drink?' asked Mia tongue in cheek.

'No,' laughed Uschi in mock-horror. 'Nothing that forward. It was a meal in a crowded Turkish bar... and of course, no snogging. In a quaint sort of way it was lovely to be courted without immediate pressure.'

'We had a terribly long engagement because Rahim had visa trouble,' Mia shuddered at the memory of it.

It was so relaxing to talk freely with someone who understood.

It wasn't that marriage to a foreigner was drastically different – her husband was westernised, held down a job and made every effort to blend into the social scene when required. However, in private, it was like living in a different world: There were lots of little things every day which took her by surprise, which were alien, which were sometimes downright unfair or illogical. She knew she had to put up with it. Her mother hadn't shown any sympathy when she had broached the subject and had rebuked her instead with: 'You wanted him!'

She wouldn't have dared to approach her husband with her concerns for fear of offending him and being called disloyal as he had done in the past.

Mia diplomatically gathered her sons before five o'clock to take them home.

'We had a wonderful afternoon. Thank you!'

Mia's friendship with Uschi deepened; they drew close in the warmth of their mutual understanding and agreed that the pressures would probably have been worse had their respective in-laws lived anywhere nearby.

The women needed each other in a society which didn't exactly ostracise them but regarded them with caution and shook its head at their foolishness, waiting for it all to go wrong. They learnt to laugh about it, feeling stronger together, supporting each other in less happy days. Occasionally they treated themselves and their children to lunch in the little restaurant just across the road from the playground.

¤   ¤   ¤   ¤   ¤

'We'll be in Turkey for about a month,' said Uschi sometime in spring.

Mia missed her friend dreadfully for six endless weeks.

'We shall be away for Christmas,' Mia announced in autumn of the same year. 'It's the best time to travel weather wise.'

'Will there be Christmas in Bangladesh?' Uschi asked tongue-in-cheek.

'I wouldn't have thought so. It's a Muslim country. But I shall try to make it a special day for the children. Imagine a palm as a Christmas tree and curry instead of turkey!' Mia joked, but didn't feel humorous at all.

It was Uschi's turn to miss her friend at a time when she was trying to get into the swing of festive feelings in spite of her husband's reminders that Christmas really wasn't for him.

They had come to a truce for Amina's sake; with great reluctance Kamal had agreed that Uschi could put up a modest Christmas tree; he would be out with his countrymen for most of the bank holidays which would give Uschi an opportunity to play Christmas carols and to give presents to her little girl.

It would have been so nice to share a few hours with Mia, her kindred soul. Uschi was trying to imagine her friend decorating a palm and cooking curry. Did she feel lonely, too?

¤   ¤   ¤   ¤   ¤

When Mia returned from Bangladesh it took her a while to be able to talk about the visit. Uschi waited patiently and abstained from prying. When Mia finally opened up, the words came like a torrent:

'My husband told me before we left that I should forget everything I had ever known. He was right. There is no comparison; it's so different, so many people, so much noise, everybody seems to be family, everybody knows your business, no such thing as privacy, the roads are constantly jammed, one doesn't walk anywhere, you never go out without a chaperone. And it's stiflingly hot and humid!' She stopped and took a deep breath

'I can't bear the heat in Turkey either,' Uschi sympathised. 'I can't really go out during the day. So I just stay in and end up making Turkish coffee for a constant stream of visitors.'

142

'We hardly went out, and when we did, it was always in a huge crowd, visiting other relatives or meeting everyone in a restaurant or cinema.'

'I know, it's not all *Hagia Sophia** and *Topkapi Satay***. Kamal's mother always moves in with us. It's no use talking to him about it; his mantra is: Guests are a gift of Allah, so I just have to put up with it.'

'My father-in-law is a widower. He moves every three months to another one of his children.'

'Did you like the food?' asked Uschi.

'Oh, I loved it, and I brought back some recipes from my sisters-in-law. There isn't much else to do, so I learnt to cook the Bengali way. The servants were horrified,' Mia added. 'They were afraid I would steal their jobs.'

'I can do some Turkish meals. Would you like to try some day?'

'We could even invite our husbands.'

Uschi was not convinced that that was a good idea, but she kept quiet.

'Let's first practise on each other.'

And so they did: One week they sat around Uschi's kitchen table and ate stuffed vine leaves with yoghurt; a week later, Mia produced lamb curry, *dhal* and curried cauliflower with potatoes. Whenever they could spare the time they took it in turns to cook for each other and their children. When Mia taught her friend to prepare *chapattis* and *parathas* they involved the children who happily kneaded the dough, bashed it flat and flung it into the hot pan, flour flying everywhere.

---

*   Blue Mosque
**   Ottoman Sultans' Palace

'Shall we risk it?' Mia asked again. Her husband had been suspicious about their close friendship. If she invited Uschi and her husband for dinner he could get to know them and stop worrying. With some luck the men might even strike up a friendship of sorts; after all they had a lot in common: for a start, they were both living in a foreign country, were both married to local women and came both from Muslim countries.

Uschi still thought it might spoil their easy-going relationship but she kept her concerns to herself and, against her better judgement agreed and accepted Mia's invitation.

¤　¤　¤　¤　¤

The woman who opened the door was not the Mia she knew: Dressed in a dark blue *sari* with white embroidery, a white blouse and sparkling sandals; her neck and ears gleaming with gold jewellery and her arms covered with bangles up to the elbows; and the make-up, bright red lips and *kohl* around the eyes – Uschi was shocked about Mia's transformation.

'He insisted that I dress up,' she whispered as Uschi walked past her. 'Keeping up the family standard!'

Uschi felt rather frumpish in her favourite beige twin-set, a tweed skirt and a modest one-rowed pearl necklace, a present from her husband on the birth of their daughter.

They were introduced to Mia's husband Rahim who appeared a little haughty, his profuse, jolly welcome sounding insincere.

Uschi had to admit that he was good-looking in a Bollywood film star manner: fiery eyes, moustache neatly trimmed, his thick black hair falling in a controlled rakish fashion onto his forehead and a sparkling smile which didn't quite reach his eyes. He was tall with broad shoulders, not an ounce of unnecessary fat on him. His physique was underlined by immaculately tailored light-grey trousers, a white shirt, a tie and a summer jacket in the same shade as the trousers. He didn't look as if he was at home but rather at a celebrity event.

Uschi began to feel sorry for her husband.

Kamal was a little shorter than her (which was not astonishing as she was exceptionally statuesque). He actually didn't mind his protruding belly because it bore witness that they ate well. His dark hair had thinned a little and was cut in the old fashion, short, back and sides.

He had always prided himself that he made an effort to adapt to life in England, hence he had dressed like an Englishman would have done for the occasion of a simple meal amongst friends: in his best jeans, a clean white shirt, a V-neck sweater and his most comfortable loafers.

Mia had given no indication that the hosts would be dressing up in finery.

The evening began with stilted conversation, a feeling of unease spreading itself between the diners like an unwelcome smell. When the food was served the conversation progressed to forced compliments and insincere praises; it wasn't the best Mia had ever produced. The atmosphere improved gradually as the men warmed to each other and began to talk about their love of all things oriental.

The women moved their chairs closer to each other, sighed and indulged in relieved giggles and whispers. The tension had made them both tired and they were glad when the men decided that it was appropriate to end the evening.

'See you Thursday?' Mia said furtively to the back of her parting friend.

When they met again on Thursday in the playground, something had changed and the conversation flowed thickly like treacle.

'Your husband is really nice; so westernised,' Mia said hoping to disguise a guilty feeling as thoughts of her husband's disparaging criticisms rang in her ears.

'And yours is terribly dishy,' joked Uschi with a naughty, uneasy grin.

They both knew that the meeting had not been a success and that there wouldn't be a repetition. The two males had been in too much competition, showing off about their backgrounds, their religious fervour, their political stances, their efforts to adapt to life in England or to preserve their own culture in a foreign country – they would never want to be friends.

The women couldn't explain why the incompatibility of their husbands put a damper on their own friendship, each becoming sensitive to the other's remarks. Soon their meetings dwindled and they began to avoid each other.

In private they met their husbands' dripping of unflattering comments about the other couple with silent contradiction and outrage which was eventually supplanted by doubt and a slow dawning that their other half might have a point.

Although the women missed each other's company they accepted that people always drifted in and out of one's life and that their friendship might have run its natural course.

¤   ¤   ¤   ¤   ¤

This relaxation of their bond freed up spare time which they filled with unconscious sadness and yearning – for what, they knew not.

It also left them vulnerable to proposals they might have otherwise fought.

'We are moving to Bangladesh,' Rahim announced, and Mia chose a little card with a sweet kitten on the front to let her friend know.

'What about the promise to your parents?'

Uschi didn't get an answer. Mia didn't have the patience to tell her about the battles, the arguments and tears. As usual Rahim had won and Mia's misgivings were ignored: Her husband had secured the approval of his English employer to open a company branch in Bangladesh. Her parents had more capitulated than agreed. They were no match for their determined son-in-law.

'Kamal has been pestering me for years to return to Turkey,' Uschi wrote again as if to keep the trickle of communication going, 'but I'm not well; I certainly can't take the heat anymore. Last summer I came out in bumps, and just thinking of being indoors all day, making small talk with his sisters – I would die of boredom!'

Mia felt that her friend's marriage was heading for a crisis but she was too busy with her imminent departure to get involved:

'Just a quick note…why would he want to leave a perfectly good job, a nice flat and a loving family? He goes to Turkey every year for a visit anyway,' was all Mia could think to write.

These were exactly the arguments Uschi herself had used all along – without success. Her husband had simply come to an age where he wanted to go home.

Mia and Uschi met one last time in a local shopping mall to have a coffee. They tried to recapture the essence of their friendship so that they could carry it forward as a much needed constant in an otherwise uncertain future. They dreaded being separated by thousands of miles.

'You know, I think I should change Kamal's diet. The older he gets the more ardent he becomes.' Was Uschi trying to lift the gloom of their imminent separation?

Mia looked at her with incredulity, but finally burst out laughing and countered: 'I wish mine had a bit more of that.'

'Be glad that he isn't pestering you all the time. When I refuse he is like a stroppy teenager for days. I think he is looking for a reason to break away.'

Poor Uschi, Mia thought and hugged her friend good-bye: 'I am going to miss you.'

'We did understand each other well; and every time I thought I couldn't stand it any longer, you came and cheered me up.'

'Good,' said Mia briskly. It was time to go and get rid of that lump in her throat. 'I'll send you my address as soon as we are settled.' It was a consolation of sorts.

¤   ¤   ¤   ¤   ¤

At first their correspondence flourished. Mia described her new life in vivid colours: It was all very exotic, magnificently exciting and thrilling.

Then the daily grind took over, Mia's husband threw himself into his new professional role; the servants had been selected; presentations and introductions into Dhaka society had been made. Boredom seeped through every line Mia wrote and eventually she admitted that she was trapped in a golden cage. Her life had ceased to be glamorous and the slow passing of each day was paralysing.

Uschi could not imagine life by-passing her vivacious friend.

'I am dying of suffocation! I am starved of mental and physical stimulation! There is always someone or some rule managing to suppress my spirit. My sense of adventure has evaporated, and I have trouble presenting a smiling face to my children. But then, I look at the poor people outside my window and scold myself that I should count my blessings.'

Uschi couldn't blame her friend for this outburst.

'Couldn't you find some hobby or charity work?' she suggested.

'I am not allowed out without a chaperone, and in our family women are not supposed to work whether for money or voluntarily. We are expected to be happy to look after our husbands and children. But then, there is not much to do in the house either because the servants get cross if I take over their chores. At least the boys seem happy as long as Mummy and Daddy are together.'

'Why not come back for a visit?' Uschi wrote hopefully.

'Can't. I am not allowed to fly on my own and Rahim has no interest. He is happy in his new job. What about you visiting us in Bangladesh?'

Uschi's husband thought this idea ludicrous:

'You can't even tolerate the heat in Turkey!' which was true.

The friends had reached a cul-de-sac once more, and over the following months their efforts to stay in contact fizzled out. It was what their husbands had hoped for; it was much safer if the two women did not influence each other.

Spurred on by her friend's courage, Uschi relented and agreed to settle in Turkey. Her husband was more astonished than pleased but accepted that she wanted to make an effort for his sake.

However, the stay went disastrously wrong: Uschi fell violently ill before she could detect that her husband's affections had strayed during previous visits.

Nobody could figure out what was ailing her, so she was flown home to England for specialist treatment. Several days of tests revealed that she had a rare and obscure allergy to sunlight and that her eye sight had deteriorated dramatically. Nobody could explain the pain in her lower abdomen. After weeks of inconclusive attempts at diagnosis and more rest than medical intervention, Uschi was discharged.

A letter from Mia announcing that she had at last managed to get permission from her husband to visit her parents in the company of the children and a sister-in-law unsettled Uschi more than it elated her.

Mia was shocked to see her friend hardly able to lift her feet off the ground, fighting for breath after every sentence she spoke. The curtains were drawn in every room to keep the sunlight out, as Amina, now a pretty young girl, whispered to Mia before leading her to her mother. The two women had a coffee and a piece of cake bought from the bakery.

'You didn't bring the boys?'

'Next time. I first wanted you all to myself!' Mia tried desperately to sound cheerful.

'How are they?'

'Getting spoilt rotten by their grandparents!' The cheerfulness fell flat and was squeezed out of the room by Uschi's struggle to breath.

'You should get a second opinion,' Mia pleaded but only earned a shrug. Mia would have loved to drag her friend back to hospital to do battle with the consultants and to nail Uschi's condition. There must be something that could be done!

Uschi shook her head.

'How is Kamal?'

'Fine, I think.'

'What do you mean?'

'He has bought a franchise and opened a business in Ankara.'

'What?' Mia shouted in disbelief. 'He left you here on your own in this state?'

Uschi was too worn out to feel anything either way. When she got her breath back she said quietly:

'I can't stay with him there. The climate would kill me. I have been told to avoid the sun.'

Mia hardly dared to ask: 'Have you thought of divorce?'

'Many times,' the answer was surprising, 'but who else would have me?'

Mia was appalled at her friend's low self-esteem. Kamal obviously just had his wife where he wanted her, waiting faithfully for him while he enjoyed as much freedom as he liked in another country.

Strangely, Uschi still felt compelled to defend him:

'He does send money to pay the bills and visits every so often.'

Mia was speechless and after another half an hour of stilted and halting conversation, she felt that Uschi wanted her to go. She said good-bye desperately hugging her dispirited and defeated friend.

¤　¤　¤　¤　¤

Three years later Mia decided that her efforts at adjusting to life in Bangladesh had been a failure. She hated the sluggish, lethargic and chubby woman she had become. She could not imagine spending another forty years leading this useless, pointless, aimless life in the lap of luxury.

When she felt that her influence on her children was slipping away because their father was bribing them and tugging at their heart strings; when their religious upbringing threatened to alienate them from her, shutting down their young, open minds, so that they would only want to be traditional Bengalis rather than cosmopolitans; when they malleably professed that they wouldn't mind turning to professions their father had chosen for them;and when her husband had started to lash out at her and her attempts to free herself from his stultifying control; having taken stock and made comparisons of the positives and negatives of her life, Mia decided that it was time to escape;

She took advantage of another official visit home and never returned. She was surprised that there were no repercussions from her husband. She suspected that she had become a liability and embarrassment for him, and that rather being surprised and saddened, he might be relieved to be free to pursue a future of his own liking.

This was closer to the truth than she could have anticipated: Soon after their uncontested divorce she received news that he had married into Dhaka High Society and planned to have more children.

¤　¤　¤　¤　¤

Once her life had moved to calmer waters, Mia made it her priority to look up her old friend Uschi. She couldn't remember the telephone number, so she set out one spring afternoon to stroll down the busy road to the Victorian house. She admired the silhouettes of the still leafless trees lining the pavements, their bare branches reaching up towards the pale blue sky and milky sun. Even the cold breeze gave her pleasure.

She found number 36 easily, climbed the stairs and rang the doorbell. When nobody answered, she checked that the little brass frame underneath the bell still displayed the same name. Strange!

The silence was broken by rustling and movement behind the door. It opened the width of a hand and the half hidden head peeping out was not familiar.

'Oh I am so sorry. I wanted to visit Mrs. Ulmat.'

'I am Mrs. Ulmat.'

Mia was confused:

'Uschi Ulmat?' she asked tentatively.

'No, she died a year ago.' said the woman in a foreign accent, 'I am only here to sell the flat.'

'Where is Amina?'

'With her father in Ankara.'

Mia sat down on the stone steps outside and cried into her handkerchief: for Uschi, her unhappiness and the lost opportunities to be a better friend to her.

It took Mia a couple of days to find out that Uschi had been buried in the graveyard near the children's playground where they had first met.

She put a bunch of spring flowers on her grave. This was not the homecoming she had expected.

And how dreadful for Uschi's daughter Amina! Brought up in the West and now having to adjust to being a good Muslim daughter. It didn't bear thinking about.

'I hope she will at least get a good education!' Mia prayed fervently at the grave.

Suddenly Mia knew what her friend would have wanted her to do: 'I shall watch over her,' she sobbed, 'I promise!'

In her mind, Mia had already worked out her strategy:
- Go back to no 36 and get address and phone number in Ankara;
- Phone Kamal and Amina;
- Visit them in Ankara; exciting for the boys, too.
- Invite Amina to come over during school holidays;
- Offer to house and care for her once she will go to university (the stepmother would probably be grateful);
- Keep the channels open at all times!!!

JAMES

JAMES

James's mobile rang, shrill and demanding but he couldn't get to it; it was in his jacket pocket hung up behind the driver's seat.

It seemed to take ages until the answer service kicked in and the grating sound stopped. Everybody knew that he was on his way to the airport, so what could be so urgent?

He pulled in at the next service station.

'We must talk!' was the message from his wife Salima.

He had only left her half an hour ago – he had held her face between his hands, had kissed her gently on the nose and stroked her long, black hair. She had looked upset but he had promised to ring her every day of his business trip whenever he would be near a phone or could find a mobile signal.

He pressed the button which dialled his home number automatically.

'Hallo?' He heard her gentle voice with a hint of the exotic.

'Darling, you called? I am almost at the airport.'

There was a pause.

'What's the matter? I am listening!' he urged her.

'I want a divorce.' It didn't sound like a demand; it sounded more like a sad and dispirited conclusion.

'What?' He could hardly breathe with shock.

'Salima, I'm sure you don't mean that! You are upset. I know I have been away a lot, but I can't help it. Look, I shall make a big effort to contact you every day one way or another. Three weeks will go quickly and then I shall make it up to you.'

'I won't be here.'

'That's nonsensical, Salima! Go over to my parents; it's only a ten minute walk; they will cheer you up.'

Silence.

'Salima, it's not fair to spring this on me now. I am on my way to Africa. Please, don't do anything. We shall talk about it when I am back. I must go now otherwise I miss my plane.'

A click indicated that she had put down the receiver.

For a minute, James sat still to regain his composure.
Then he put the car in gear and slid slowly back onto the motorway.

He, the Head of the Government Trade Mission, just reached his colleagues as they were chaperoned through the business class lounge and accompanied to the aircraft. As soon as he was seated he took papers out of his briefcase and leafed through the pages, but he couldn't concentrate. Salima's words kept ringing in his ears. He closed the report.

No point dwelling on recent developments, he thought. He would have to deal with them on his return.

Instead he cast his mind back to the first time he had met her.

¤   ¤   ¤   ¤   ¤

Three years ago, she had been the sweetest apparition in his entire life; her smile had lit up her face as if he was the most welcome guest of all. He had been one among many of a Trade Delegation installed very comfortably at the Taj Palace Hotel in New Delhi. When their official negotiations had come to an end they were invited to go on a tiger hunt.

He declined. He had reports to prepare for the London Office and wanted to catch up on sleep before boarding the plane for the long flight home. Moreover, hunting was really not his thing.

That's when he met Salima, one of the reception staff. He had needed a breath of fresh air and had thought of combining it with a bit of sightseeing. It turned out that she was free the next day and they arranged that she would be his guide.

'Would you like to go shopping for your family?' she asked lowering her eyes.

He laughed and assured her that he had only parents and a sister who didn't expect presents whenever he travelled.

It being India, she insisted on bringing along a chaperone, It turned out to be her younger brother, Shamim, who eyed him with suspicion.

They hired a baby taxi which took them to the busy Connaught Place, one of the largest commercial areas in the city; on it rattled through the kingly Rajpath Avenue and past the black marble cenotaph of India Gate, erected in honour of the fallen Indian soldiers in the Afghan wars and World War I.

The atmosphere was jolly: On the lawns around India Gate people met, chatted or had picnics.

James was impressed by Salima's knowledge of local history and observed that she was in her element.

'You are a very good guide,' he commented.

'I love history but I don't know enough,' she replied smiling shyly and lowering her eyes as if she had spoken out of turn.

Soon James' head was swimming with the names of Laxmi-narayan Temple; Humayan's Tomb, the first of all Mughal monuments; the Qutub Minar, the first monument built in India by a Muslim ruler; and the Raj Ghat on the bank of the Yanuma River, the final resting place of Mahatma Gandhi.

They asked the taxi driver to stop, and James realised, catching Salima's horrified look, that he had vastly over-paid him. To stretch their legs, they took a leisurely stroll through Shantivan, the 'Forest of Peace', where India's first Prime Minister, Jawarhalal Nehru was cremated.

They hired another baby taxi to take them back to the hotel, passing the North Block, where James had had most of his dealings with Government officials, and the Rashtrapati Bhavan, the presidential palace, where he had once been invited during an earlier mission.

Brother and sister were most impressed. The furthest they had ever got to were the gates.

By the end of the day, James was smitten by his guide and he couldn't wait for the next day to meet her again.

They did not manage to see the magical sunrise from the Taj Mahal, but after they had disembarked from the airless, sticky late morning train they had enjoyed the magnificence of the palace, a tribute of Shah Jahan to his beloved wife Mumtaz Mahal. They spent the day wandering through the geometrical gardens and along the stunning lakes and water features, heat and beauty spinning a web of silky dreams, until they had to leave.

As they arrived back at the chaotic Delhi Central Station, James put much warmth and gratitude into his words of thanks. They made her smile, and she beat a hasty retreat lest he should get carried away. Within seconds she had disappeared amongst the crowd, her younger brother trailing sulkily behind her.

James was disappointed not to see Salima at reception the following morning and was informed that she would be in for the evening shift. By then, he would be well on his way to the airport. He left a brief message and his address in England which he feared might end up in the waste paper basket under the desk.

◻ ◻ ◻ ◻ ◻

He hadn't heard from Salima for three months when he decided that she either hadn't been given his last communication or she didn't really want to keep in contact.

Either way, he needed to know because for some reason her lovely vision refused to fade and the memory of her gentle smile still warmed his heart.

'Can I please, speak to Miss Salima Roy?'

The Taj Palace Hotel receptionist was unimpressed.

'She is not here at the moment. Can I help you?'

James explained that indeed he had to speak to Miss Roy personally and was finally and unwillingly put through to an office.

'Salima Roy speaking,' his heart leapt as he heard her voice again.

'It's James, James Cummings.'

'Hello, James.' It didn't sound quite as enthusiastic as he had hoped.

'How are you? I haven't heard from you, so I thought I give you a ring.'

There was a long pause as Salima wrestled to find the right words: 'James, this is my last day at work. I am getting married. So, I can't write to you. I am sorry…'

His heart stood still.

'Can't it wait?' Why was he asking such a silly question?

Salima didn't reply.

'Do you know your future husband?'

After another pause she replied: 'My parents have chosen for me, so he will be a good man.'

James's worst nightmare had come true: This beautiful Indian girl who had occupied his dreams for weeks would soon be married off to a man she didn't even know never mind loved. He felt sick when he thought of another man's hands on her.

'Salima, I missed you and I would like to see you again. Do you feel the same?'

'I don't know.' Her voice trembled.

'Please, wait; I shall be with you in four days' time and we shall talk it over. Will you try to stall your parents for me?'

'I shall try. I can't promise.'

They had arranged to meet after his arrival in the lobby of the Taj Palace Hotel. She looked even more ravishing in her green sari speckled with tiny metal discs like space dust glittering in the sun. For the first time he saw that her black hair, which when on duty she had twisted into a chignon, reached down to her waist. She looked elegant and sophisticated and her smile was as lovely as he remembered.

They felt self-conscious in the hotel, so they went down the road for a meal. Both were picking at their food without interest, realising that they had reached a momentous point in their lives.

They finally agreed that the next day she should introduce him to her parents.

'Why?' she had whispered.

'Can't you guess? I have to ask your parents for their permission. Are you happy with that?'

She nodded in slow motion and hope spread all over her face.

¤　¤　¤　¤　¤

Salima's family lived in a less salubrious part of town.

He felt like a school boy in front of the headmaster sitting opposite her parents, Salima squashed between them on the settee. He could hear children giggling in the corridor behind the door curtain.

At first they talked stiffly about England, politics, then his family and job. They didn't give much away about themselves.

'May I invite you all to dinner tomorrow night at the Taj Palace?'

This seemed to go down well, and it was agreed that he would send a car from the hotel.

It left him the morning to buy a matching set of gold necklace, earrings and bracelets.

The evening was a great success. Salima's father, sitting next to him, slapped him several times hard on the back which he took for approval. It gave him the courage to push back his chair, stand up, raise a glass of mango juice and ask for Salima's hand in marriage.

¤　¤　¤　¤　¤

The three days of wedding celebrations tossed him around as if he were in a tumble dryer. He was overwhelmed by noise, colour, food and masses of happy people, guiding him from one place to another, telling him what to do or not to do. He was getting hungry at awkward moments, when it wasn't time for eating. He had to shake off sleepiness and replace it by good humour and good manners. All he was waiting for was Salima's radiant and reassuring smile that they were not committing the folly of the century – but she was nowhere to be seen.

When she was finally led towards him in her red and gold sari, his heart almost burst with love, pride and happiness that she would be at his side for the rest of his life.

¤　¤　¤　¤　¤

On their flight to England Salima had been torn between the excitement of beginning a new life abroad and the pain of leaving everything and everybody she had ever known behind. Soon her adventurous spirit won out.

During the first months of their marriage he was given a period of grace: someone else took over the travelling. The young couple's life turned into one round of parties, dinner invitations, theatre and concert visits and a couple of official functions. He had every reason to be proud of her. Not only did she look absolutely stunning in the *saris* she insisted on wearing, she also proved to possess instinctively impeccable manners. Her graceful style and never wavering diplomacy were much admired. If she wasn't sure about what was expected of her, she smiled, observed, copied or, if more appropriate, withdrew and melted into the background. She couldn't have been a better asset to his position.

As they settled into their new home, James discovered that he had married a natural hostess who was not only charming but also had a flair for interior design and an unexpected talent for cooking. Their Indian dinner parties became well-known and sought-after. James would come home to wonderfully exotic smells wafting through the house, and he would imagine for a moment that he was back in India.

In spite of their loving and often passionate relationship Salima didn't conceive. She refused medical tests and rather prayed to Parvati, one of the Hindu Goddesses of fertility.

When her longing for a baby became apparent, James bought her a puppy, not realising that this was a mistake. He was taken aback by her disgust that she should share her lovely home with a dirty creature she had been brought up to loathe. He took the little fellow to his sister and her three children who were delighted with the new arrival.

In the second year of their marriage, he was sent on several assignments abroad which took him away from her for three weeks at a time. In spite of invitations from his parents and friends, Salima grew bored and lonely.

'Could I work in a hotel like the Taj?' she asked him on his return.

'You don't need to.'

This was not how he saw the role of his wife.

'Can I study?'

James bought her a computer to take part in on-line courses. She decided on completing her education and enrolled for A-levels in English, Maths and the three Sciences.

'Don't overdo it!' he admonished her but he could see that she was happy, and that was good enough for him.

It took her two years and she passed with flying colours.

'I would like to study medicine,' she announced but he felt unhappy about it.

'You don't realise what you let yourself in for. Look, sooner or later you will have a baby, and you won't have the time.'

In truth he was scared that he was about to lose his gorgeous wife to a career and the wider world.

The next time he came home, a little earlier than planned, he found a group of young people in his sitting room, discussing courses and lecturers. Salima ushered them out as quickly as was decent seeing her husband's thunderous face. He felt like an intruder in his own home.

There was something else different about her. With a sudden shock he realised that she had cut her beautiful hair to a bob with the fringe just touching her eyebrows; she also had exchanged her *sari* for a pair of jeans and a white blouse tucked into it. She looked slim, curvy, even sexy, but nothing like the demure girl he had married.

'You have changed,' he commented bitterly and went to bed before he had the chance to say something he would regret in the morning.

When he came down for breakfast, she was just finishing a phone call.

'You don't need to make calls behind my back!'

He saw tears in her eyes: 'I cancelled my course at Medical School,' she said simply wiping her tears away.

'Why don't we plan a holiday after my next trip?' he tried to sooth the pain.

'Can we go and visit my family?' She brightened up immediately.

'Darling, I am on so many flights all year. Can't we go somewhere we can drive to, like the West Country?'

The light went out of Salima's face but she agreed; she hadn't seen much of England apart from the county she lived in.

The trip was a disaster: It rained most of the time and Salima turned out not to be a fan of pebble beaches and a freezing cold sea. She found the cliffs frightening and as they crossed Dartmoor on their way home, she declared it 'the bleakest place on earth.'

This was a disappointment to James who had hoped that she would share his spirit of adventure and memories of childhood summers.

They consoled themselves with meals in exclusive restaurants run by celebrity chefs but returned home deflated and both developing colds.

¤ ¤ ¤ ¤ ¤

Divorce! He couldn't believe it: His precious wife wanted to leave him; his exotic dream might soon come to an end.

As soon as the plane landed in Johannesburg James tried to ring home and left a message. He tried three more days between meetings, but never got an answer. He rang his parents who assured him that they had invited their daughter-in-law for dinner on the evening of his departure. She had seemed subdued but they had blamed it on his absence.

'I shall go round and check,' offered his mother but he didn't want to worry her.

'She has probably gone to visit friends,' he said but in his heart he was not convinced.

James was getting distraught and his colleagues noticed. In the end, he invented a pretext about ill-health in the family, handed over the leadership of the delegation, rearranged some meetings and booked an early flight back to England.

Sitting on the airplane, James had plenty of time to think. Like many men, he hadn't read the signs; he thought that his wife had every reason to be content. Little disagreements were normal in relationships, but when he reflected on his marriage, month by month, it dawned on him that his behaviour had been crassly stupid: He had uprooted her, installed her into his world like an exotic prize and had kept her in a gilded cage; he had expected her to cope with a vastly different culture to the one she had grown up in and to get along with people who were well-meaning but had different values than the ones which had

167

been drummed into her; he had never been there to help her, to explain things, console her when adjustment had been hard.

And worst of all, he had stifled her, had ignored her ambitions and had wiped out any prospect of personal fulfillment. Had he really assumed she didn't need it? Most women in the western world did.

The clarity of this conclusion hurt: No big house, luxury car or enough money to buy anything she wanted would be enough to compensate for her sense of abandonment.

It was ironic that he had wanted to save her from an arranged marriage and then had behaved just like an Indian husband – clipped her wings just when they had begun to grow.

He was ashamed and remorseful and vowed that he would make it up to her.

¤   ¤   ¤   ¤   ¤

He shivered in the cold drizzle which welcomed him at Heathrow airport. He was dishevelled, exhausted and desperate to put his good intentions into action.

When he turned the key in the lock, he realised immediately that Salima had left – the soul had gone from their beautiful house. The colourful cushions with the little mirrors sown into them had vanished from the beige settee; the dining room table was polished, the chairs were tucked under and new candles had been put in the candlesticks, as if the cleaner had just left.

The kitchen sink was gleaming, the Shaker-style cupboards were spotless; only the little vase on the breakfast table with its reduced smelly water and three stems of dried up roses, whose petals had fallen onto the surface, indicated that Salima had been away for several days.

Finally he saw it, a piece of paper on the fridge door, held there by a magnet which said: *It's never too late to be what you might have been.*

The message was short, in unsteady handwriting and dotted with smudges.

Dear James,

I have gone away, not to India, my parents would be ashamed of me. My college helped me to transfer to a course in America. I want to become a doctor and then go back to help my people. It's hard to fit in with your lifestyle and your idea of marriage.
I am so sorry. You have been good, kind and generous and I am grateful for everything you have done for me.
I can't expect you to understand.
Please, don't follow me; I won't return.
Take care.

Salima.

James put his face in his hands and cried, realising that the kindest thing was to let her go.

¤　¤　¤　¤　¤

Five years later he found out by chance that Salima had indeed caught up on her education and that she had been accepted at Stanford University, California. She was aiming to become a paediatrician. His heart, although still aching, swell with pride and he admired her from afar like a secret lover.

By then he was living with an English girl, a friend of his sister, who had brought a toddler into the partnership. He tried to travel a little less, but Jackie didn't seem to mind one way or another. He reckoned that he was happy, as happy as he would ever be.

ANASTASIA

ANASTASIA

'No, you are not going to marry him!' Her father's voice was steely to indicate that that was the last word on the matter.

Hella was distraught. She really loved her new boyfriend Oskar. Admittedly, he was considerably older than her – to be honest by more than twenty years – but he was youthful, charming, interesting, lots of fun and – not that it mattered – rich.

She was determined to talk her parents into accepting him, to give them every opportunity to find out how wonderful he was. She would work out a strategy; she would win them over and marry him!

'Can I invite him for lunch sometime?' she asked her father who was peering at her with narrowed eyes whilst her mother, a shy, cowed woman, stood behind him smiling nervously.

'No, he is not entering this house!'

What was wrong with her parents? They had been hostile from the moment she mentioned Oskar's name. She had only told them the bare minimum about him, and as far as she knew, they had never met him.

'I want you to give me one good reason why you don't want to meet him.' Hella didn't really care about a reason; all she wanted was to change her father's mind.

'Where shall I begin…' he said sarcastically, ending with a disparaging 'ha' like a triumphant exclamation mark.

'Is he a criminal?' Hella demanded to know.

'Not exactly.' Her father seemed to get irate and his answers ever shorter.

'Is it because he is too old for me?'

'Of course, he is!' She would have liked to point out that Oskar was a lot more active and informed than her much younger father would ever be but now was not the time.

'Is that it?' It was so unfair!

'No. We have made enquiries' Her father turned to go.

'Is he married?' Hella persisted.

'N-o.' It was a long drawn-out syllable which made Hella suspicious. Did they know something she didn't?

'Is he?'

'No' this time a sharp, exasperated shout.

'So what is wrong with him?' Hella wanted to get to the bottom of this. 'Tell me!'

'You ask him; it's not for me to say,' he spat the words out.

'And what shall I ask him? Whether he has any idea why my parents dislike him without ever having met him? They accuse him of something but they don't know what? Is that what I should say?' The words tumbled out; her eyes blazed with fury. She had to take a deep breath.

Silence ensued during which all parties seemed to examine the floor.

Where had their warm relationship and trust evaporated to?

'Ask him why he was a member of the Nazi party.'

The sentence hung in the air like an acrid cloud.

Hella was bewildered and for once, stunned into silence.

¤　¤　¤　¤　¤

She carried this monstrous accusation around with her for more than a week and pretended not to notice Oskar's worried glances.

'What's wrong?' he asked one evening after dinner in his apartment. He gently held her chin and tilted her head so that she had to look straight into his eyes.

There was no point in denial.

'Why would my father call you a Nazi?' Her eyes pleaded to tell her that it wasn't true.

'Aha!' Oskar stiffened and moved a little away from her. 'I thought it might reach your ears.'

Her eyes widened and she hoped she had misheard.

He placed his hands on her slim shoulders, squeezed them gently to press her into the nearest arm chair.

'We better skip going to the movies and talk about this,' he said. 'I'll make us a pot of strong coffee; I have a feeling that we shall both need it. It will be a long night; it's a long story.'

¤　¤　¤　¤　¤

Oskar Hoffmann was brought up in Vienna in the 1920s. His father owned a chain of public swimming baths; his mother was a beautiful socialite and a brilliant hostess. They lived in a big old Patrician house in the middle of town.

175

The family also owned a holiday home on the foothills of the Alps so that they had the choice of either sailing on the lakes or skiing in the mountains.

Oskar's parents gave big parties and when home from boarding school, he met many of the celebrities of the time: Sigmund Freud, the psychiatrist, Walter Gropius with his Bauhaus ideas, Albert Einstein, who shambled through the party crowds, the actress Annie Ondra, Zsa Zsa Gabor, more known for her scandals than her acting, a young Billy Wilder, the film maker, even Charlie Chaplin came once briefly and the unofficial king of New York and baseball star, Babe Ruth was a regular visitor whenever he was in Europe.

Towards the end of the thirties, many celebrities from the arts withdrew and were replaced by people like Engelbert Dollfuss, the then Chancellor, and Richard Suchenwirth who had founded the Austrian branch of Hitler's National Socialist party in 1926.

Oskar was glad to be away most of the time as a boarder at Schloss Salem College. He knew he was privileged to be at a school for the children of the noble and the wealthy. He liked the atmosphere and ideals of its founder, the educator Kurt Hahn and thought it a scandal when, a few years later, under Hitler, the poor man, on account of being Jewish, had to flee to Scotland.

Oskar passed his Maturum* and went on to study medicine at Heidelberg. However he soon discovered that this was not for him, and he ended up being taken into his father's business.

'My parents joined the Nazi party quite early on,' Oskar explained to Hella, 'and they urged me to do the same. Unfortunately, I had taken a dislike to them; the party members were far too fervent for my taste and had the strangest ideas about the future of Germany and its people, particularly the ones they didn't think were German enough. I wanted to keep out of it, but my father was adamant and tried to pressurise me. It ended in mutual embarrassment and I was soon excluded from their social life.

---

* A Levels

There was one memorable row during which Oskar told his father: 'I don't know what you see in that poisonous little man who wants to take over the world.'

Of course, it didn't go down well. Soon afterwards, Oskar was dispatched to a family friend who had a similar business in Stuttgart. There he was given an important-sounding position but not much scope for doing anything. His father had simply called in a favour.

His new boss, Kurt Baeuerle, was a rotund man with a florid complexion and sharp eyes. He was always dressed in a three piece suit and wore highly polished fine leather shoes. He ruled his staff with an iron rod but treated Oskar with much kindness. Oskar didn't feel he deserved it as he wasn't of great use to the company. He enjoyed far too much free time which he spent reading in his bachelor pad or making new friends in clubs.

Occasionally Oskar was invited for dinner to Kurt's house where he met Ana, his wife. She spoke with a slight foreign accent – haltingly as if trying to hide it – and after serving dinner she often retreated to leave the men to their own devices. Oskar had no idea what Kurt's opinion was on the political developments; to his relief they were never discussed.

The young Oskar loved these evenings with his boss; somehow Kurt seemed to understand his ideas and hopes a lot better than his own father. Oskar slowly became the son the Baeuerles never had.

The idyll changed when Kurt fell ill and needed a life-saving operation. Oskar went to visit him in hospital. To his surprise Kurt asked him outright whether he had ever joined the Nazi party.

Oskar shook his head and remained silent. He thought it a strange topic to bring up in the circumstances.

'I take that as a no then, shall I?'

Oskar looked at the patient, pleading for leniency.

'I have to ask you a big favour,' Kurt continued.

Oskar was pleased to be finally of proper use to this kind man: 'Of course,' he said with eagerness.

'You know my business – not so different from your father's. Most of it is common sense anyway, and you are a bright young man. So while I am stuck in here, I want you to take it over. I am sure you will make a success of it.'

Oskar felt dizzy at the prospect of running Kurt's empire of public swimming baths but how could he refuse?

'I shall do my very best,' he promised and added: 'while you are recuperating.'

'There is something even more important,' continued Kurt. 'It is a huge thing to ask a young man of your age but there are not many people one can trust nowadays. I trust you!'

He paused, catching his breath: 'I hope it will never come to it but should I not get any better,' he paused as if to summon up strength to ask the question: 'Will you look after Ana?'

It was the first time that he had not referred to her as Mrs. Baeuerle. Oskar was not entirely sure what Kurt meant, but before he could ask, the explanation followed: 'You know how the Nazis are becoming more and more powerful and dangerous; they keep asking me to join the Party; so far I have resisted. I fiercely disagree with their policies particularly with their relentless persecution of the Jews.' Kurt sighed, and the two men smiled at each other in mutual understanding.

So his boss had known all along about his lack of enthusiasm for the regime.

'I guessed when your father sent you hurriedly to me. And I have decided that should anything happen to me I want you to be the one to look after my wife, to be there for Ana, to protect her. You see,' and here he paused as if frightened to utter the words, 'Ana's real name is Anastasia and she is a Russian Jew.'

178

'This explains the accent,' Oskar thought; he had never quite been able to place it.

Anastasia, Oskar learnt, had fled as a seven year old during the 1917 Revolution with her parents from Petrograd*. They had left their charmed life behind and had fled across the continent disguised as beggars; it took them almost two years to reach Stuttgart. Anastasia had always smiled remembering that when the family had arrived that June, the whole of the town seemed to be a garden of roses and she had pleaded with her parents to stay.

The family had hardly settled in when the father had died; it had all been too much. Anastasia and her mother were left and had to try to make some sort of living. The mother had always been sickly, so the task to provide fell to her young daughter.

'That's how I met her,' Kurt smiled at the memory. He seemed exhausted and lay back on his hospital pillow.

¤　¤　¤　¤　¤

Oskar put a glass of water to the patient's lips.

'She came into my office as a fourteen year old and asked for a job. Of course she was too young, but I kept her on to do errands, make tea, keep order. Then I sent her to commercial college. She was absolutely brilliant! So hard-working and intelligent! In time, I promoted her to be my PA; I soon couldn't do without her and trusted her implicitly to deal with all parts of the business. And then of course, we fell in love!' Kurt laughed out loud as if he had pulled off a brilliant ruse.

'We went out for a couple of lunches together; then dinners, and finally we met up on Sundays as well. Of course, these meetings always had to be short because Anastasia had to rush home to look after her mother. When I proposed she turned me down at first. 'I can't leave my mother,' she had said, so I realised that I would have to buy a big house to accommodate them both.'

---

* now St. Petersburg

179

'We have a lovely life together!' Kurt mused. 'During the years of our marriage, Anastasia has been a wonderful wife, a wonderful companion, my best friend. With her help the business grew from strength to strength. We now own not only the company but also five houses in town.'

Kurt coughed and had another sip of water with Oskar's help. There was some more he was eager to explain: 'And through it all she has remained modest; she has never forgotten what her family went through and how badly wrong it could have gone. She once said that she would be forever grateful that I had taken her in. I don't see it like that at all. I am the one who is in her debt for the years and years of happiness!'

Kurt sunk further back into his pillow and closed his eyes, whispering: 'Think about it, Oskar, and let me know your decision. I must be sure that she will be safe!'

¤   ¤   ¤   ¤   ¤

Oskar had never really taken much notice of Anastasia beyond the courtesies of a guest. As he left the hospital, he tried to picture her: Taller than Kurt, slim, almost ascetic, a mane of red, curly hair, green eyes, always elegantly dressed; one thing he remembered particularly: her long, slender hands like those of a concert pianist. She was an excellent cook and a charming but unobtrusive hostess.

It wouldn't be difficult to take care of her.

He was never told what had ailed Kurt but after a few weeks in hospital, Anastasia took him home to care for him herself. He died not long afterwards.

Kurt's last will put Oskar at the helm of the Stuttgart swimming baths empire. Business matters diverted the new director's attention away from the widow.

However, political developments threw them together sooner than expected: After *Kristallnacht* and rumours of Jews being resettled in the East, Oskar told Anastasia about her late husband's request.

180

'I don't want you to get into trouble because of me.' She looked at him with concern and without self-pity.

By then Oskar had forgotten about their age gap and had grown very fond of her. Like Kurt, Oskar could now not bear the thought of losing her.

For thousands of *Reichsmarks*, Oskar had a passport forged which changed Anastasia's name officially to Ana and her place of birth to a little village in the Black Forest. It turned her overnight on paper into a locally born, devout Catholic woman.

'We shall marry', he said with enthusiasm. 'Then nobody can touch you.'

They exchanged marriage vows at the local registry office. It was a moment of pure bliss in a world full of inhumanity. Anastasia looked as happy as any young bride.

As the rumours of extermination camps in the East grew frighteningly stronger, the couple weighed up the pros and cons whether to give in to the pressure of joining the ruling party or not. As a now prominent entrepreneur, Oskar was approached regularly by officials, and every time he made a huge donation to pacify them.

How could he become a Nazi being married to Anastasia?

The *Wannseekonferenz* in 1942 rubber-stamped the Final Solution; investigations into people with Jewish ancestry were accelerated and deportations to the Concentration Camps became a daily occurrence. It was frightening and took the decision out of their hands.

Oskar joined the Nazi party, and, in order to explain his wife's invisibility, invented a story that she was an invalid. This excused her from attending party functions and public events.

The association with Nazi officials gave Oskar advance warnings whenever raids of Jewish houses were planned. It enabled him to move Anastasia from one safe house to another. They played a constant game of cat and mouse which Anastasia bore with fatalism. She knew that it was necessary for her survival. Oskar hoped fervently they might just get away with it in the chaos of war.

He kept the swimming baths open until it became impossible. They felt lucky that only one of their town houses had been bombed.

After Germany's defeat in 1945, they settled back with relief into a quiet life, and Oskar tore up his Party membership. It had always burnt a hole into his pocket but it had done its job..

¤ ¤ ¤ ¤ ¤

'That's why your father called me a Nazi,' Oskar ended the story and his nervous pacing up and down the sitting room. He looked pleadingly at Hella who had not interrupted him once.

'My poor love!' She got up, stood on tiptoes and took his face between her hands. It was her turn to make him look at her.

'You are a hero, Oskar! I hope you know that! So where is Anastasia now?'

'She died four years ago. I buried her next to Kurt.'

¤ ¤ ¤ ¤ ¤

Hella and Oskar were married in September 1964 with her parents present. The only problem the newly-weds encountered was that they couldn't spend their honeymoon in America as planned. Oskar was refused a visitor's visa 'due to his affiliation during the Second World War.'

'Then we don't ever want to go there,' said Hella with spirit. And so it proved: they travelled all over the world, but never to the United States.

My aunt Hella is now eighty-five and Oskar is long dead. She still loves him!